# ATTACK

Little
DOZEN
press

Attack

Published by Little Dozen Press
Stevensville, Ontario, Canada
www.littledozen.com

Cover design by Mercy Hope
Copyright 2015

ISBN: 978-1-927658-31-4

# ATTACK

BOOK 3 OF THE ONENESS CYCLE

by Rachel Starr Thomson

Little Dozen Press

2015

"You have never talked to a mere mortal. Nations,
cultures, arts, civilization—these are mortal, and their
life is to ours as the life of a gnat. But it is immortals
whom we joke with, work with, marry, snub, and exploit—
immortal horrors or everlasting splendors."

—C.S. Lewis, The Weight of Glory

## Pulsing white light.

Heat.

A smell like earth, and like something burning.

Richard opened his eyes and stared at the ceiling. His room was quiet in the heat of the night. A ceiling fan, clacking slightly, whirred overhead.

He didn't know what the images meant, or the smell. He'd been awakened by them three times in one night.

He got up and stretched, staring out his window down toward the bay, sparkling in the lights of the marina. There was no moon tonight—the lights of the harbour were all that illuminated the water. The town, stretching down the slope to the bay, was mostly dark. A few lights here and there indicated that someone was up or someone was nervous, leaving lights on to discourage unwanted visitors.

The town did not often have reason to fear. But since April

had caused the death of an intruder in their own house, just under Richard's bedroom, and Chris and Tyler had come home injured, rumours had been spreading.

And something more than rumours—a feeling, an atmosphere that was instinctive, spiritual.

Defending themselves against the hive's attacks had been nearly deadly.

Tomorrow the offensive began.

Tomorrow they split up, but not in disunity. They had a plan to carry out.

It was so hot.

The ongoing march of summer, worse inland than here in the village.

Unexpectedly, Richard found himself thinking of the hermit on Tempter's Mountain. He had given his life for this war. Lost it to one who should have been an ally, and closer than an ally. To one who was Oneness.

Richard's own cell had been so fortunate thus far. They were all still alive. There was no guarantee that fortune would continue.

But one thing he knew: they could not allow the wounds that David and others had pierced in the Oneness to fester. Whatever they had to do, whatever it cost, they had to heal the breach.

\* \* \* \* \*

**Rachel Starr Thomson**

Reese awoke reeling still from what she knew. She had seen the exile as about herself, always—the pain of it so overwhelming that there was no option to see it as anything else.

She had not seen it for an attempt to destroy the very Oneness itself, an attempt to infiltrate and infect, to bring the darkness and the demonic into the very fabric of that which held the world together.

In all her years of chasing the hive, she had not dreamt that the hive's target was not just the people inhabiting the world but the Oneness itself. That they weren't just going after networks, but after The Network.

She knew it now.

She breathed in the air slowly, inhaling bay salt, humidity, a cool breeze that wouldn't last long in this summer day. The breeze died away even as she began to appreciate it.

The sun, having risen, was already turning the day into an inferno. It fell through her window in beams that heated the bed and weighted her down.

She breathed in again, taking in the stiffness of the air, the calm before the coming storm.

Today everything would change, and this time, it would be the Oneness that changed it. Not the hive. Not David. Not even the circumstantial workings of some invisible plan.

She would get up in a few minutes and walk into that work. For now, she lay here. The day was intimidating.

She soaked up the quiet.

Despite the heat it was only, maybe, six in the morning. The house was silent. Others were awake—she could sense it. Sense them worrying, thinking, planning, praying, though no one had risen from bed. One or two dreamed. Tony, she thought, and Angelica. Young and brash and willing just to charge into whatever came, hang the consequences. She was grateful for them. Grateful they'd stuck with her, that they'd come along after her to join this tiny cell and its wild, everything-changing plans.

She smiled in the sun rays and the salty air.

A slight knock on the door. Someone was up after all. Strange that she hadn't sensed that.

He pushed the door open, and it was Chris. Her heart beat wildly, and she sat up and pushed hair out of her face and pulled her sheet up to her neck. He was not supposed to be in her bedroom. Irregular enough that he was in the house, seeing that he was not Oneness and had no business, strictly speaking, being so in the middle of everything.

He flushed, but he didn't move from her doorway. She noticed that he wasn't looking at her—being a gentleman, then, even if he was standing in her room first thing in the morning.

"I thought you'd be awake," he said.

"Well, yeah."

"It makes sense that Richard's splitting us up—I get it, even though I was mad at him for it last night. We both need to go where we're going. I just want you to know . . . well, be careful, please."

Her voice was strangely strangled in her throat. Lately his nearness did this to her. "I will." She cleared her throat. "You do the same."

"I can take care of myself."

Yeah, he could—he was a big strong man, young but full of good sense and good character, just like his father. And his father had died, a long time ago, trying to protect people he loved in the attack that had birthed all of this. The attack that had started fracturing the Oneness years ago, before anyone was aware of it.

Her eyes said some of what she was thinking, and he just grunted in return.

"Listen, do you . . . uh . . . want some breakfast or something? I can bring you . . ."

She almost swung her legs out of bed and then remembered she wasn't entirely dressed. "We can eat downstairs. Get out of here and I'll get dressed and come join you."

He flashed her a grin and disappeared, leaving the door slightly ajar so she could hear his retreat down the hall.

She got up, rolling into the thickness of hot air, and closed the door and pulled clothes on, difficult to do over the cast on her ankle. She grabbed her crutches and blew out a sigh as she stared at the door and the day on the other side of it.

Oh, Chris, she thought, Come in. Come into the Oneness. Come in where I can love you, and you can love me, and we don't have to do this anymore.

But she wouldn't say any of that.

The others joined them one by one, trickling into the kitchen over the course of an hour, putting on coffee when they finished the pot Chris made, making tea, scrambling eggs and frying bacon. No one really talked. Mary and Richard came in first, then April, then Shelley and Nick—together. Diane, who had probably been awake quite a while but didn't want to dive into the day before she'd had more time to think and process or just avoid them all. Tyler and the twins last. Fully half of them looked like they had recently lost a fight. Chris and Reese were the worst, with their casts—Reese a snapped ankle, Chris a broken arm. The hive did not play nice.

At least they were all still alive. That was a miracle in itself.

They ate without really talking and cleaned up just as quietly. Those who were Oneness—all but Chris and Shelley and Nick—felt each other's tension and simply shared it. The others watched them, wide-eyed, knowing that a great deal was happening beneath the surface.

They gathered in the common room when they'd all finished eating. Nick sat himself between Richard and Mary and looked up at them each in turn, his eyes wide and his expression solemn. He clutched his sketchbook and pencils, but they were shut; he'd been working on something but not showing it to anyone. April sat beside his mother.

Everyone waited.

"If anyone has more to say than we've already said, now's your time," Richard said.

"Go get them," Nick said.

"Be careful," Shelley put in.

Richard smiled. "Thank you. Both. You can pray for us while we're gone."

Shelley looked skeptical. "We ain't like you."

"But you can be," Richard said. "The door is open. You only need to step through it."

She didn't respond. Richard looked over his people, his cell, his family, and felt a swelling of pride and the edge of concern. They had already been through so much.

But there was no turning back now. Not now that they understood what was happening. Not now that the attacks had coalesced into a coherent picture, one that called upon them to stand up and fight back.

They said their good-byes and split into teams, going their separate ways.

They did not know when they would come back together. Or if they would ever come back together.

The attack had begun. They went out to seek their targets and bring them home.

Reese and Tyler after Jacob, the community leader who had opened his trusting people up to the demonic and had in some way killed a man.

Richard, with the twins, after the children who had been set free from possession, so that he could talk to them and try to find out something about the rest of the hive: how many more there were, how many might be Oneness, how many they needed to name, recognize, and rescue.

Mary, April, and Diane after the most volatile of all, with Chris helping them.

They were going after David.

The source of it all.

The place where the wound had opened.

The first exile.

* * * * *

It was David that Reese thought of the entirety of the drive to the correctional facility where Jacob was being held in custody along with his wife, kept for questioning and until charges could be made. David she puzzled over, David she ached over.

David had been the head of the Lincoln cell as long as she had been there. She had known him as a leader, a father—a head. The Oneness were all connected, all becoming part of each other more tangibly the longer they lived together, and somehow, for years, he had kept it up. Kept up the connection while hiding his hatred and anger and bitterness, hiding the scheming and the demonic contacts, hiding the truth. And for all those years they had loved him and cared about him as their own souls. That he was an enemy worse than any demon or outsider was still, even after all she had seen and heard and been attacked by, almost unbelievable.

It seemed like a bad dream, one conjured by too many nights of poor sleep and bad food, that you could only wake up from and shake your head at and be glad it could never, ever be true.

She wanted to confront him herself. She wanted to be part of the team that was going after him, and perhaps to find the part of herself that was still missing and become fully Oneness again in the process.

That desire was why Richard hadn't let her go after David. Why he had said she should focus elsewhere, and she knew he was right. It was too personal, for her. She would lose her head. She would make decisions based on her own needs and not on the needs of others. She would be a liability.

Part of her still hated David for that. She had been guilty of nothing he accused her of. The exile had been a sham, a facade, an illusion cast by his own alienation and pinned over her. And yet it had changed her. She was less than she had been; she was unreliable where once she could have been trusted to the grave. And it wasn't her fault.

She sighed heavily and leaned her forehead against the window, hoping the glass would be cool as they drove over blazing asphalt on their way to the city.

The glass wasn't cool. Pressing her head against it only made her feel more closed in.

Mirages rose from the road ahead of them. Diane's air conditioning worked only intermittently. They were using her station wagon. Tyler kept casting furtive glances at her from behind the wheel.

"Are you okay?" he asked.

"Yes."

She knew he knew she was lying.

"You know," he said, "I wondered why this whole story felt so much bigger than us. Like why, in the beginning, I kept seeing your old friend—Patrick—and April saw one of the cloud, too. They don't usually come, do they?"

The cloud were those members of the Oneness who had died. Their connection was never lost, so they remained part of the family, part of the organism that now crossed heaven and earth. But no, it was not common for them to appear or participate in any way the others could see.

"No," was all she said.

"But it makes sense now. Now that we can see David is targeting the whole Oneness—all of us, all over the world. Maybe he could even get to the cloud. Imagine what that would do to the world."

Tyler was new to the Oneness, and things that were understood by the others still amazed and impressed him. But Reese had to admit she hadn't thought of that one.

Could David's hive really reach into the cloud? Start turning even the departed against those on earth? Could the infection spread that badly, that virulently?

She suspected it could.

"This Jacob," Tyler said, continuing to talk as he barrelled down the highway, "he really confused me for a while. He's got so much personality and power, like Richard. And his community—they are really . . . special. Just innocent and wanting to make a good life for themselves, you know? Wanting to do what's right."

"Lots of people have good intentions," Reese said. "But foundations matter a whole lot. If you get those wrong, you can't build anything good on it. Jacob should have been building on the love and unity of the Oneness, and he chose to build on fear and control instead. Nothing really healthy can come from that."

"Do you think there's a way back for them? His community, I mean?"

"Yes," Reese said after a moment. "If they're looking for Oneness, they'll find it. Especially now that the truth is coming out. They should be able to get free of him."

Unless the truth just destroys them, she thought, thinking of the girl Miranda and her mother, and the young men who had already been sucked into demonic practices—if Miranda's version of events could be trusted. Could they really come out of all this unscathed?

No, she decided. Not unscathed. Never that.

But healed. Eventually, somehow, they could find healing and reality where they'd been bound by hurt and illusion.

"I didn't tell anyone, but I think maybe I saw angels when I was at the house," Tyler said. "They were sitting in my hospital room talking about the community and how they looked like Oneness, but they actually weren't. And they said some things about love and what makes humans different."

Reese looked askance at him. For someone who had hardly been Oneness for any percentage of his life, Tyler had already wracked up far more unusual experiences than was normal even for one of a long-standing cell. "Angels? Are you sure you weren't just on drugs? Angels are not common things to see."

"Neither is the cloud, and I've talked with one of them quite a bit."

"True." She smiled. "Tyler, do me a favour. Stay safe through all of this. They gave us the easy job—the protected one, with prison walls on all sides—so we wouldn't get hurt. So just abide by that, okay?"

He chuckled, but she sensed something behind the laugh— memories, fear. "No worries. I'm not the one who rushes off into trouble. That's you. Or Chris."

"But trouble seems to have a knack for finding you," Reese replied. She waited for him to say what was bothering him so deeply. He didn't.

Not that she couldn't guess. He had been there when the young man, the European one they called the Wizard, whose real name was Clint Wagner and whose background check had turned up a frightening record—had ripped two policemen apart with his own hands. He had seen it, or at least heard it. That he wasn't a basket case was a miracle. And he had nearly been burned alive in the hive's attempt to turn Diane.

And to turn her. Reese.

"Are you okay, Tyler?" Reese asked quietly.

He didn't answer her right away. Outside, the world was blurry in the heat. He was sweating under the effects of the inefficient air conditioner.

"I tapped into something back there," Tyler said, "when the hive still had us. The strength of the Oneness. I walked under that strength when I should have been paralyzed—literally got up and moved legs that should not have moved, all through the energy of people other than me. I think, right now, the Oneness is still holding me up. If I try to go under them to myself, I'm still . . . not in a good place. But I'm not alone. That's keeping me together."

"That's more self-insight than most people have," Reese commented. "Even Oneness."

"So how about you?" The direct question caught her off guard. "You are still dealing with a lot. I know that. You lost the Oneness—lost what's keeping me together. Do you feel like you've come back?"

"No," she admitted, unable to be dishonest in the face of his honesty. "Not really."

He nodded. "I'm sorry."

"It's not your fault. I just need . . . time."

"Do you wish you were going after David instead of the others?"

That question rattled her too. Yes, she did. David was the front line. David was the prize. He was the one who mattered most, and Reese had never liked being away from the front, away from the charge. She knew that Jacob was also important, that they had to go after the hive in any incarnation where they could find it, but she also knew she was being sent to him because it wasn't personal, and she wouldn't be safe if she went after David. Even though Mary had her own history with him, she had been judged safe, and worthy, and able to do this, and Reese had not.

That stung.

At the same time, it was a tremendous relief.

Because she knew they were right.

"It's best that I go where I'm going," Reese said. "Richard is right about this. I don't like it. It's hard. But he's right."

Tyler tried a smile, but it came to more of a grimace. "I'm sorry," he said again.

They drove on, and then he laughed.

"So we're on the attack, and we're starting by going to a jail and trying to talk to someone. Just talk. And hope he listens and cares enough to turn around. What in the world kind of war do you fight like that?"

Reese smiled grimly. "The only kind there really is."

She settled back into her seat. "But you're wrong about one detail. We're not just going to talk."

He looked startled. "What? What else would we do?"

"We're going to break him out."

"We what?" There was a squeak in his voice. She heard it in his spirit, too—a racing to try to keep up with her.

"I know Richard wants us to stay safe, but Jacob is not going to come back to us while he's sitting in prison," Reese said. "He needs to come out and be with us. Alongside us. Where we can reach him. So we'll most likely have to get him out. Besides, the prison doesn't know what they're dealing with. It wouldn't be safe for him to stay there."

"Because he's dangerous?"

"Because right now, he's spreading a hive. And prisons are already swarming with demonic activity. If he gets in there and gets that bunch organized, things may get very, very bad."

"Oh. Wait, we're not going to go fight some kind of huge battle all by ourselves, are we? Why didn't the twins come with us if things are so bad in prisons?"

"We might be. We'll win. Keep your eyes on the road." He was starting to swerve, clearly hugely distracted by the sudden change in how he was envisioning this battle playing out. "Trust me, Tyler, we'll be all right."

She tried to sound confident. A prison full of demons, she could handle.

Jacob, she wasn't sure.

**Richard arrived at the children's home** in Brass and greeted Dr. Smith, who was waiting for him by the front door and had it opened before Richard even got a chance to ring the bell. He'd come in a rental car, having loaned his to the group going after David.

"Welcome," Dr. Smith said. His eyes shifted from Richard to the twins. "Is this all of you?"

"Everyone is deployed," Richard said. "We already know our main target. They've gone after him."

Dr. Smith nodded and ran a hand over his bald head. "Thank you," he said, abruptly. "Thanks to all of you for how much you've already sacrificed. I don't fully understand what you're doing, but . . . well, I have two children in this house who I think owe you their lives."

"That's more true than you know," Richard agreed. "May we see them?"

"Of course. Come in. My wife will make you coffee."

"No need. I just want to see the children."

The doctor nodded and squared his shoulders. "Well, come with me. They're in the office. Are all three of you coming?"

"I thought that might be overwhelming. The twins can stay out here. Perhaps talk to Alex."

"That's what I thought too." The doctor looked relieved. "Forgive me if I seem overanxious. These kids . . . they're in a bad way. Nightmares and frozen up, just not wanting to talk at all. I've never seen so much fear in any child's eyes. And I've seen a lot—a whole lot." He paused. "But they want you. They've asked for you. What did you do for them?"

"I loved them," Richard said. He smiled sadly. "Just held their hands and did my best to father them. Like you do. And it got through enough that they wanted to break free. But I know they've been badly traumatized by everything." He paused. "You said Alex is here too?"

"Under house arrest, yes. We promised the police we could keep him contained."

Richard looked concerned. "That might not be true. He's still got . . . company."

"The company is behaving, so far. I figured you would want to talk to him, and you could do it more easily here than if he was at a facility. We just want to be of service."

Richard stopped just before Dr. Smith opened his office door. "Before you leave me with the children—I just want to say thank you, sir. You've been more help than you know."

Dr. Smith nodded and smiled. Then he opened the door.

The children were waiting, sitting side by side in chairs with their hands clasped. A boy and a girl, brother and sister, just a year or so apart in age. The boy was older, maybe twelve; the girl eleven.

When they saw Richard, both their faces flooded with relief, then flashed fear.

"It's all right," Richard said in a low voice, and moved more than he had expected to be, he opened his arms and embraced both children like a father.

They were supposed to be his undoing. In the attack, David had appointed them, possessed as they both had been, to hang onto Richard's hands. He knew Richard wouldn't hurt them— and their demons would afflict them as soon as he tried to do anything against David's plans.

It had worked. For a little while.

But children were still children, and these were frightened, lost, needy children who were desperate to become part of a different story than the one they found themselves in. So Richard had held their hands as tightly as he could without hurting them and had willed them to know that they could be loved, and protected; he had reached out with everything in him, spirit to spirit, calling to them with Oneness and with Spirit and with fatherhood.

They'd heard.

It had worked.

They had cried out for deliverance, and Mary had driven the demons away.

But they were even more lost now. Tormented by memories

and fears, with minds like empty rooms where other powers had occupied, desperately needing to be filled.

He was here to learn from them. To ask them about what they had seen and heard so he could find out if there were others like Jacob and David: members of the Oneness who had turned against the body, who were working with demons to build the strength and numbers of the hive, who were trying to destroy themselves by destroying the Oneness.

But he wouldn't ask them questions yet.

He held them close, pressing them both to his chest, and found himself weeping.

They clung.

* * * * *

His name was Jordan; hers was Alicia. They were twelve and eleven. They had parents, to Richard's surprise. The children had no idea where those parents were. They'd been raised by a grandfather who liked to dabble in the occult. They could not say exactly how or when their own doors had been opened to the demons. Only that it was fun, for a little while, and then terrifying and awful, and they had wanted nothing but to get away.

Richard listened to their story—mostly Jordan talked—and wished the last part was true. But he knew it was not. Those who got a taste for demonic power rarely wanted nothing but to get away: they were afraid, yes, but also addicted and drawn.

His love had broken through to them. He hoped it could stay that way. That they would not be drawn back.

The one way to ensure that was to become Oneness. But they would have to enter—to Join—of their own accord. In the same way they had opened themselves to the demonic, they would have to open themselves to the Spirit. He could do absolutely nothing to make that happen. It was nothing any human being, no matter how spiritual, could control. He could only love them. Draw them, by the power of love.

So he told them about the Oneness. He told them there was a family, a body, connected as a single living, breathing organism across life and death, times and dimensions, millions of threads holding the entire universe together in the power of one unifying Spirit.

To be One, unlike being possessed, was not to possess great power or independence. It was to be a servant, responsible to everyone. But it was also to be embraced in a hold deeper, higher, greater than fatherhood, or romance, or family.

They were twelve and eleven. He didn't know how much of what he said connected, how much of it even made sense to them.

He marvelled, even as he spoke, at how these things had shaped him. He did not often think about that. The Oneness was his normal. It had been for decades. He could hardly conceive of life anymore without it. But as he spoke, he remembered himself before the connection, the Joining. He remembered how the Oneness had changed his life.

It was no wonder the rebels could do so much damage. The Oneness was not a small thing. It was everything. They were trying to destroy everything.

When he finished telling them all these things, he hugged

them again and said, "You're safe now, here."

Alicia nodded, her small head rubbing against his shoulder. Jordan didn't respond.

Then he sat back and looked at them both again. "I need your help," he said. "The Oneness needs your help. Will you give it?"

"What can we do?" Jordan asked, suspicious.

"You can just tell me what you know," Richard answered. "Anything you learned while you were part of the hive—about what David was trying to do."

"David hates you," Jordan announced. Then immediately looked fearful of his own brashness.

"I'm sure he does. But who else does he hate? Who else was he going after? Who else was he working with? That's what I need to know."

The children exchanged a look, and Richard sighed. "We're going to do our best to keep you safe," he said. "You don't have to be afraid to tell me."

"We're not afraid," Jordan said, but his eyes told a different story.

Alicia didn't bother to confirm or deny anything. She just sat silently and trembled.

Richard waited, but neither child spoke.

He wondered if they didn't, after all, know anything. Or if they just weren't willing to tell.

"Did you know Jacob?" he asked.

Jordan hesitated. "Clint did."

"Yes," Richard said. "Clint went out to see him."

"Clint went to spread the hive on Jacob's farm," Alicia said. "Usually he came back and just laughed and laughed. He said they were stupid and just walked right into it."

"Was there anyone else like Jacob who Clint went to see?"

They were silent. Stone faces.

He chose his words carefully. "Did they threaten you if you tell?"

Both children returned stares. They weren't blank—but he couldn't read them.

Richard picked up the narrative again. If he could just tell the story, maybe they would chime in—correct him, confirm something. "Clint is possessed, and he went out to the farm to get others to open up to the demons too. And they did. Jacob helped him. And Clint had other places he would go to do the same thing. People listen to him because he's powerful, and they want that power."

Still stone faced.

"There are others like Jacob and David—men or women who are Oneness but are angry or hurt or just want to control, and they invite Clint in. And he would go to them like he went to the farm . . ."

"No," Alicia said.

Jordan shot her a dirty look.

But the expression in his eyes was becoming clearer—clear enough that Richard could read it.

It wasn't fear.

It was guilt.

"Not Clint," Richard said quietly. "You would go to them."

"To her," Alicia said.

"To her. Who is she? Where is she?"

They didn't answer his questions. "David told us we were like the Oneness too, but better," Alicia said. "He said we were helping to set people free from it. He said that's what the demons were doing."

"You knew he was wrong, didn't you," Richard said.

"The demons don't help anyone with anything," Jordan said. "All they do is wreck stuff."

But there was a note of triumph, of power, in the way he said that. Richard heard it and shuddered deep inside.

He hoped, desperately hoped, this boy would come into the Oneness. Otherwise, it was only a matter of time before he let the demons back in.

Human beings were not meant to exist on their own. They were meant for spiritual connection, to be part of a fabric. Once they had connected, either to the Spirit or to the demonic, they could not go back into isolated independence forever.

"You're right," Richard said. "Demons can't help anyone. And they can't make people like the Oneness. All they can do is control and try to force everyone to be the same. That's not Oneness."

They were retreating back into their shells.

"So," Richard said, clasping his hands, "tell me about her. Please."

*　*　*　*　*

Lieutenant Mitchell Jackson met Reese and Tyler at the prison. To their relief, he told them that he'd been able to keep Jacob separated from anyone else.

"Was there some kind of trouble?" Tyler asked.

"No," Lieutenant Jackson said. "But I don't want him in with anyone else. The man is more kinds of trouble than I can think about. He makes me want to listen to every word he says. Last thing I want to do is throw him in with a bunch of criminals."

"You're wise," Reese said.

"How does a man come by that much influence?" Jackson asked. "His sneezes have more authority than my orders."

"It's a gift," Reese said. "One he's misusing."

"Pardon me, but he's one of you, isn't he?"

The question hung in the air for a minute. They hadn't told him about themselves—who and what they were.

"I know you're not just . . . normal," Jackson continued. "I've seen a few things in my life. Learned there are powers out there that aren't just human. Including you. You're not the first ones I've run into."

Reese nodded. "You're right."

"And he is one of you?"

"He is," Reese said.

"I've never seen one of you go bad."

"We hadn't either. It's not normal."

"So you're here to what? Get him back? Discipline him? Hold an execution?"

"Lieutenant," Reese said with half a smile, "what exactly are you going to do with my answer to that question?"

He lowered his voice. "Quite honestly, I'm going to let you do whatever you're here to do. I'm out of my league. You take this out of my hands, I'll be more than grateful."

"Isn't that going to get you in trouble?"

"Depends on what you do. I'll find a way to keep the heat off myself as much as I can. I just want you to deal with this."

"He killed a man."

"Maybe he did. Nothing is proven. His wife swears it was an accident; I think I believe her. She's a bitter old hen, but I don't think she's a liar, and I don't think she would kill anyone." He paused. "You want her too?"

"Not right now," Reese said. "She isn't one of us."

"If you don't mind my asking . . . what exactly are you?"

"We're Oneness," Reese said.

She knew that didn't answer his question at all.

But she couldn't really go into more right now.

He nodded and led them in. Through two sets of security, and finally into a room with bare white walls, a table, and three chairs. Jacob sat on one side. He wore his own clothes—a button-up shirt and work pants—and his hair and beard were neatly trimmed. His eyes flashed fire as they sat down.

**Rachel Starr Thomson**

"You can't keep me here," he said. "I am guilty of nothing. They will have to see that and let me go."

"You're guilty of a great deal," Reese said, "but we don't want to keep you here. Actually, we want to get you out where we can talk to you properly."

He looked up, smirking. "You're saying that in front of their cameras."

"We're okay."

"You're working with the police on this?" A tiny bit of his smug confidence wavered.

"They are servants," Reese said. "Like we are. Like you are."

He sat back and folded his arms. "And you are here to what? Chastise me for failing to serve properly? You hardly deserve the name Oneness. Any of you. You have a high calling, and you've failed to live up to it."

"You, on the other hand, are a faithful servant of God," Reese countered. "Failing to bring any of your followers into the Oneness and opening them up to demons instead."

He flushed. "What you call the Oneness is a perversion of itself. I am building the purified assembly, the Oneness as it is meant to be."

"With demons?"

"Have you considered that you might be wrong about power?" Jacob asked, clearly on his own footing again. "That what you call angels and demons may be falsely so-called?"

"You brought Clint in to introduce your people to his kind of power. What kind of betrayal is that?"

"He is a man of God."

"He ripped two men apart with his hands," Tyler said quietly. "I was there. And he tried to burn me alive, along with my friends. He uses witchcraft. What part of that is of God?"

Jacob's face hardened. "You only see what your eyes tell you. You can't see the reality, the Spirit behind the flesh."

Reese buried her face in her hands. Not to hide, but to control herself—her own anger. To try to get in touch with an answer. The man was insane. She didn't know how to respond to him.

And he was one of them—so much one of them. She could feel his presence, burning and powerful, like her own heartbeat.

That made it all so much worse. He was a brother. Passionate, totally given to his convictions, very much like her.

She wanted to embrace him and kill him at the same time.

Behind her hands, she knew what to say. She didn't move them as she spoke.

"Where did we fail you?" she asked. "Where are you hurting?"

He laughed at her. "What do you think I am, some little boy having a tantrum because somebody hurt his feelings?" His voice grew steadier, more authoritative. "Tyler, you were on the farm with us. You saw the community I was building. The good we were doing."

"I saw people afraid to be who they were," Tyler said. "Good people—people with dreams. But you asked too much from them."

"I did not. Holding people to a high standard is only right. How else were they to become who they wanted to be? How else could they leave the world behind and grow to their full potential as servants of God? There's nothing evil in our community, Tyler. You saw that."

Reese looked to the side and saw that Tyler was looking straight into Jacob's eyes, uncowed.

"I saw a man abusing his gifts," Tyler said, "and turning his back on his real family. That's evil. And I saw him welcome the demonic into a place where he had promised to protect. That's evil."

"I told you," Jacob said, "you are wrong about what you believe about the demonic. The Oneness is wrong. We've compromised too much—gone too far. We don't know the difference between right and wrong anymore. We don't know the difference between the power of God and the power of darkness. If we did, you would know that nothing I have done has been wrong."

Something in his gaze made Reese lower her hands.

"You accuse me of turning my back on my family," he said. "I have not done that. I am trying to purify my family. I care about the Oneness. I care more than anything in the world. That's why I've taken the road I've taken. That's why I sit here in prison and endure persecution. It has not been easy for a moment. But I have to walk this road."

And Reese felt shaken. Because he meant it. Because he believed every word he was saying. This wasn't David, duplicitous and scheming to the core. This was a man convinced of the rightness of his own actions.

And completely, utterly, destructively wrong.

"All right then," she said slowly. "You believe we are wrong—

that we've bought into a perversion of the Oneness. We believe the same about you. I'll accept that you have to walk the road you're walking. So I'll make you a deal. Walk it with us for a while. One week. We'll get you out of here, and we'll do our best to help your community out of the hot water it's in. You come with us, and do all you can to show us how wrong we are. But you ask yourself, every day, if you might be wrong. And ask it honestly."

It was clear he was taken aback.

"That's not the deal I was expecting you to offer," he admitted.

She smiled. "Thank you for that honesty."

"I am not a liar."

"I believe you."

"But you believe I'm deceived."

"Deeply. Yes."

He thought about it a moment. And she appreciated that—appreciated that he wasn't just jumping on her offer, convinced of his own ability to hold out and wanting to get as much out of her willingness to help as he could. It was clear he was truly considering her terms.

"So all you're asking," he said, "is that I spent a week following you and question myself."

"You don't even need to follow us. We'll split—you lead and we follow; then we lead and you follow. You teach, and you be taught."

She wasn't really sure where this idea was coming from. It

was far from what she'd intended to suggest when they arrived. A bit ruefully, she pictured Lieutenant Jackson's likely response if he knew what she was offering. He'd been afraid of Jacob's influence. Was that influence just affecting her, and she didn't even know it?

No. This was right. It would work.

"Very well," Jacob said.

She didn't know if she was relieved or burdened that it was actually going to happen.

She did know, against her own expectations, that she loved this man as a brother with all of her heart and wanted him, desperately personally wanted him, to come home.

"Do you want us to get your wife out too?" she asked, not sure whether that would even be okay with Jackson.

"No," he said firmly. "I don't want her under your influence."

"Fair enough."

She stood. "I suppose we'll meet you outside."

"What, no show of power?"

Was he laughing at her? Teasing?

"No . . . we're working with the police, remember? No blowing holes through the walls. We'll use the door."

They left, and Tyler looked at her with eyes wider than she'd ever seen them.

"I can't believe we're doing this."

"I want him back," she said. "He's family. He's lost."

"Why do you care so much?"

"Don't you?"

"Not like you do."

She thought over the question. "I don't know. Because we're One. Because I know how it feels to be lost. To be . . . deceived. To believe with all your heart that something is true when it is not."

He nodded. "I admire you, Reese. For this. It's crazy, but it's right."

She smiled, grateful to the core for his words and his friendship. "It's the war we're here to fight. But thank you. That means a lot."

He laughed and shook his shaggy head. "You're crazy, Reese."

"So they've always told me. I'm glad you don't mind."

"Oh, I mind," he said, his eyes twinkling. "But I don't have much choice, do I? Be dragged along by the Oneness, and especially you, or else go back to life alone. No real choice at all."

Troubled thoughts clouded her eyes. "But Jacob made that choice. And David. And maybe more."

"I think you're going to bring him back," Tyler said. "I think if anyone can, you can."

She gave him a smile and wordlessly squeezed his arm.

In the old days, before the exile, she had never been so insecure.

But then, before the exile, no one's faith in her had meant so much.

**While Richard talked** to the children in the office, Dr. Smith ushered the twins upstairs to "talk" to Alex.

He was under house arrest, which amounted to being grounded in his room, and he sat in the corner and glared out at them like something they'd trapped there. Dressed in his usual all black, with his hair oily and his eyes glowering, he remarkably resembled an animal. His room, normally a picture of his inner state, had been stripped. Big blank spaces on the walls, marked at the corners with bits of tape, showed where posters that had plastered them had been torn down and thrown out. His bookshelves were empty; likewise his closet and drawers. Dr. Smith, his wife, Valerie, and the house mother, Susan Brown, had passed the point of tolerance while Alex was trying to murder the Oneness and had cleansed the room of every dark-leaning thing they could find.

As it turned out, that amounted to nearly every single item Alex owned.

The twins sat cross-legged on the floor across from him, silent, holding their swords across their laps very visibly and very much at the ready.

It was the boy, not the demon, glaring at them, but it was present, and they didn't know when it might decide it had been provoked enough and attack.

"Not exactly helping you out, is it?" Tony asked after they had sat for twenty minutes without saying a word.

Alex did not answer.

"That inner buddy of yours. The one who's supposed to give you power and all that. It's not exactly helping you out of a tight spot."

He didn't even move.

"In fact, I'd say it's pretty much leaving you high and dry. You know you're old enough to go to jail."

Alex finally opened his mouth. "That won't happen."

Angelica answered. "You're pretty confident considering that all your friends got arrested too."

Alex smiled, a smile that sent shivers up both their spines. "They can't be held."

"There's a better way, you know," Tony said. "To be human. To be empowered."

"To be like you? No thanks." He smiled again. "That loser, David, was like you. Pretty obvious how well that worked out."

"'That loser' is the reason you have your power," Tony countered.

When Alex answered, his voice had changed.

They weren't talking to the boy anymore. The air took on a chill, a poisonous edge.

"He gives us nothing. It is we who give to him. We empower him."

"He gives you organization," Angelica said, holding her voice as steady as she could. "Purpose. A plan. Without him you fall apart, just like you always do."

Alex's face sneered. "He thinks he owns us. He is a fool. It is our plan. We are using him."

"To get to us," Tony said. "To get into the Oneness."

The sneer became a smug, mocking grin. "The greatest prize. It is not so hard to make you fall."

"Sure it isn't," Tony said. "That's why you haven't won after thousands of years on this planet. That's why we're still here, still fighting you."

"Still losing."

"Still holding everything together. The sun rose today. It will go down tonight. I'd say we're winning."

"But we are turning you. One by one by one."

"Correction," Tony said. "You're failing to turn us."

"Jacob. David. Reese . . ."

"Reese isn't yours. Or Diane. They're still ours."

The grin did not move. "For the moment."

Alex's face went suddenly ashen and twisted, as though he was going to throw up, and then he was back.

Had he even heard any of that?

It was one of the worst things about demons—the way they took over, forced you into yourself and away from yourself. There was no loss of self in the Oneness. Only self-discovery, self-realization, as part of a greater whole. A whole that a hive, with all of its control and seduction, could never hope to replicate.

Alex eyed the swords still resting in the twins' laps and said, "Look, I'm not going to talk to you. So why don't you just leave me alone."

"We're concerned about you," Angelica said.

"Isn't that sweet."

"And you might need containing," Tony added.

Alex grinned. "That might be true."

His was a horrible smile. No joy. No humanity, really.

"How long have you been like this?" Tony asked.

He didn't answer.

Back to silence.

They sat and stared each other down for another hour.

At some point, the twins blinked, and when they opened their eyes, Alex was gone.

*　*　*　*　*

In the office where they were still talking to Richard, the children fell silent and then began to shake, rolling their eyes and trembling with fear, then jumped up and tried to run. He grabbed them both, looking around as though he expected something to dive straight through the ceiling and attack them. Maybe he did.

"What is it?" he asked. "What are you sensing?"

And somehow, though they were in a quiet office in a quiet house, he was shouting over a roar—a swell of noise in the air like a train coming through or an avalanche falling. The pressure in the air rose like blood, and Richard tucked both children under his wings and brandished the sword he suddenly held in his hands.

Nothing became visible. Nothing materialized. But a sound like voices, then laughter, then the boom of a cannon filled the room, and the air went darker than midnight. Richard's sword shone in the darkness.

He could hear himself shouting for the twins.

The presence disappeared.

The room went back to normal.

After a few minutes, his heart still pounding, he released the children from his side.

They were white with fear, but not shocked.

"What was that?" he asked them.

But they trembled and wouldn't answer him.

He remembered the voices, words he couldn't make out. "Did they talk to you? What did they say?"

They just shook, mutely, staring at him.

And he was calming, moment by moment, realizing he couldn't push. Realizing they couldn't talk, not in this kind of fear. Realizing the consequences might be real if they did.

"Alicia, Jordan, you don't have to tell me what you heard unless you want to. But think about the Oneness. Really, really think about it. If you come into us, we can keep you safe. We can't always save your lives, but we can help you live forever as part of us. If you don't come in, if you don't Join, I can only do so much for you. I'll do everything I can. I'll keep you as safe as I can. But there are limits."

He was pleading, not just stating facts. Most people would not ever be bothered by demons like this. But these children had seen too much. They had been too much.

For them, it had to be all or nothing.

He heard shouts outside the room. A teenage girl crying, doors slamming.

Dr. Smith threw open the door, his expression grim. "Thank God," he said. "Thank God you're still here."

"What do you mean?"

"Alex is gone."

"Gone?"

Tony and Angelica appeared in the hallway behind him. "We were in the room with him, watching him. Swords drawn. He disappeared—we don't know how. He's just gone."

Richard nodded and looked at the children with one more pleading, almost desperate gaze. "We need to get these two somewhere safe," he said.

"It's safe here . . . at least it was. I don't know . . ."

He interrupted the doctor gently. "It's as safe here as anything can be on earth, but we aren't just dealing with earth here. We need to get them somewhere with a shield." He hesitated, then lowered his voice. "And frankly, Doctor, I'd advise that you move your whole operation where we tell you to, until this fight is over. You're far too much on their radar."

"Do you have somewhere to suggest?" The doctor looked shaken, but he kept his voice calm and stood his ground.

"Yes. A place called Tempter's Mountain. An old friend built quite an impressive shield there, and it's not far. I'll take you there myself, and the twins will stay and act as extra guardians."

"I don't know if we can just move all the kids," the doctor said. "They're in summer school, and we're accountable to . . ."

"Excuse me, sir, but if you don't move them, Alex may come back and kill them all. You found the drawings in his room. You know what he was into here. He's made you all vulnerable. I'm sure you can find something to tell your supporters and the school board. Field trip. Retreat for leadership training. Something."

Dr. Smith made a noise like he was swallowing back something he was going to say. "Yes."

"How soon can you all be ready to go?"

"We'll have to get one girl out of class. Pack up. Three hours."

"Make it two. Or one."

He nodded again. "One."

"Good." Richard inclined his head toward the children in the centre of the office, staring wide-eyed at him and at Dr. Smith. "Tony, Angelica, guard these two. Swords out. Something just talked to them—whatever got Alex out, I think. And I don't know what it wanted. Doctor, if you don't mind, may I have access to your roof?"

The good man hardly even reacted with surprise.

Richard was going out where he could survey the neighbourhood, watch the sky, and pray—create as much of a shield over this house as he possibly could in the sixty minutes until they all vacated for Tempter's Mountain.

In his heart, he blessed the hermit and wished he were still alive.

He would get them all settled in, protected beneath the old man's formidable walls in the air, and leave the twins inside while he went off to seek her.

The one the children had been trying to seduce into the hive.

A woman around whom thousands more might turn.

**Of all the battles** to be fought in this war, of all the journeys to be taken on the offensive against the dark, it was Mary's and Diane's that Richard had deemed likely to be the hardest.

And the most necessary.

So it was fitting they started it here.

They stood side by side in a graveyard, a little plot of land on a slope overlooking the bay. It was ten miles from the village, a mostly forgotten little place that was kept mowed and tended by relatives of others who were buried here.

Douglas had bought the plot here himself, declaring he'd lived most of his life away from people and didn't see any reason to change that in death.

Except, Diane had often reflected, laughing and crying all at once, it hadn't been true. Douglas was a little taciturn, and very much independent and free and do-it-yourself, a man's man in a world that didn't remember what men were. He was his son's father in every way. But he had never abandoned his race. Never become a solitary, a grouch, someone who hated people and let them know it, who ran strangers off his property with a shotgun or threatened to call the police on loud neighbours. He was loyal, caring, and always looking out for others.

That was why he had opened his doors to the Oneness when they came, refugees from a massacre and a bombing and law enforcement gone wrong. When they came, running from demons that hounded their heels baying for blood, shaken and bereaved and desperate. That was why he had taken in Mary and her twin brother and his family, why he had not opposed Diane joining the Oneness though he did not Join himself, and why he had died.

Protecting them.

Neither woman had ever forgotten that night, or that man.

Chris hung back at the edge of the graveyard. He did not come here more than once a year, when he would bring his mother on the anniversary of his father's death. He had not really known Douglas. Was too young when he died. Knew that he was his father reincarnated in many, many ways, and was perhaps afraid to face the spectre of his own end here.

Or maybe he just didn't like graveyards.

April waited with him, casting furtive glances from the women standing at the gravestone to the son, pacing in the weeds outside the boundaries of the cemetery.

How different, how ironic the stories she was learning.

Douglas, who never became One but died for them anyway.

David, who was One, was still One, and was doing all in

his power to destroy them.

And both because of the same event—because of the same demonic attack.

They had learned a few things in their recent interactions with David. That he blamed Mary for his misery, because at some long-forgotten day in the past, she had brought him into the Oneness. Of course she hadn't—no one could be forced in, all came of their own accord. If he was One it was by his own choice. But he needed someone to blame, and he blamed her. That it was the demonic attack all those years ago that had turned his heart bitter and angry. That he had gone to the hermit on Tempter's Mountain seeking some way to be released, to be exiled, to be amputated from the body he had joined. And that there had been no way.

What exactly had happened to him—what exactly had caused the inferno of hurt that was threatening to devour them all now—that was still a mystery.

One they intended to solve and to heal.

If it was at all possible.

And if it was not . . .

Maybe there was one way to perform an amputation.

"Are they almost done?" Chris burst out. He kept his voice to a stage whisper, but April winced anyway and cast another look at the women by the stone.

"I don't know."

"I don't know why they needed to come here."

"It means something to them."

"Yeah. It means they've already lost too much in this fight."

"Maybe that's incentive to keep fighting."

"Maybe they're just broken and they don't know what else to do. Maybe you all are."

"Everyone is broken," April said. "That doesn't make them fools. Or without value in the fight."

He stopped his pacing. "That's not really what I meant. I'm sorry. I want to see this battle won as much as any of you. I just don't know why we have to be here."

"Do you remember him at all? Your dad?"

He shrugged. "Maybe. A little bit. I remember a feeling more than a face—a presence."

April smiled. "The Oneness is a little like that."

Then she said, "Maybe, if you'd known him, you would want to come here too. It might feel more like you were close to him."

He didn't answer. Instead he turned and stared out at the blue water stretching away just beyond the slope. Sails dotted the distance, and fishing boats closer to shore. April wondered if that was where Chris felt close to his father—on the water, with a fishing net in his hand and the sun beating on his head and shoulders.

"What about you?" he asked, turning abruptly. "You even have parents?"

The question might have sounded harsh and uncaring if Chris hadn't been Chris—if she didn't know, from watching him with his mother and Reese and Tyler, that his reason for being was to care.

"Yes, I have them," she said. She wanted to tell him more—didn't she?

No, she didn't. The Oneness had mostly let her bury the past. Better it stay that way.

"And you can remember them?" Chris asked. Far more gently now.

"Yes, I can."

He nodded. "I think they're ready to go."

She looked up. Mary and Diane were making their way across the grassy yard to her and Chris.

They were done facing the past for the moment.

Ready to go seek out David and force him to face his.

And April wondered, suddenly fearful, how many more of them would have to do the same.

Though Mary made a point of stopping to meet April's eyes and give her a sad smile before they moved on, neither she nor Diane spoke. They simply led the way back to Richard's car, with Chris falling in behind them and April trailing at the back. They'd discussed the plan before coming up here: go to the jail where David was being held in custody prior to charges—among other things of kidnapping, attempted murder, and arson—and try to talk to him, try to get through to his heart. And if that didn't work, spring him out and take him away somewhere where he would have nothing but the Oneness to fall back on, where he would have to face himself and them.

There was only one place they could go where they were sure no one would interfere—not the law, not hive members, not anyone. It was Chris who would take them there.

Out to sea.

Maybe, if he wouldn't turn, never to bring him back.

April chilled at the very thought. Even knowing they were considering it—that they were all considering executing one of their own—tore her apart to a degree she could not explain.

The Oneness was supposed to be hope, safety, a home. Not a judge and jury, not an axe to fall. The Oneness was grace and transformation as you opened yourself to the world as it truly was and embraced community, connection, becoming more than yourself and finding your place in a whole. That they would end a life instead of transforming it—

That ached.

She was afraid, too, of the consequences. The demons avoided killing Oneness. When they had to, they tried to do things like they'd tried to do to her—to trap and starve them, or cause them to fall into an accident, anything that left the blood technically off their hands. They were quite happy to inspire human agents, like those in the hive, to do the killing. But they knew there were consequences to blood. To murder. Consequences they feared. Necessary as it might be, April did not think she and the others would escape the consequences if they killed David.

But really, what other choice did they have?

They drove along the coast for a while, down out of the cliffs, and then turned inland toward Lincoln and the large city jail there. The heat of the sun grew worse the further they drove from the water. Thankful that Richard's car was new and comfortable and air conditioned, April laughed at the bitter incongruity of caring about the temperature when the whole world as she knew it was rocking on its foundations.

They knew something was wrong as soon as they arrived at the jail. Caution tape stretched around its perimeter, police officers were swarming the parking lot, examining who knew what. Bystanders had gathered, but the police shooed them off as best as they could.

Chris parked the car across the street from the jail, and Mary was out the door almost before he'd put it in park. She jogged across the road and approached the nearest officer.

"Excuse me," she said. "We have an appointment to see someone you're detaining—David Foster."

"Sorry, you can't. All visits are off."

"What's happened here?"

"That's confidential for now, ma'am."

She scanned the parking lot, taking in the activity and what looked like a scorch mark on the ground. The others gathered behind her.

"What's going on?" Chris asked loudly. The officer sighed and said again, "Confidential. Move along, please, folks."

"You lost them, didn't you?" Mary asked.

"Excuse me?"

"You lost the prisoners—the new ones. David Foster and Clint Wagner. And the rest of them."

The officer barked a laugh. "I wouldn't say we lost them so much as they just walked right out. But not all of them. We've still got Parks and Foster."

"Parks?"

"Jessica Parks. The woman who was brought in with them. The only one who walked out of here was that freak—left the others here to spite them, if you ask me."

So much for confidential. Mary kept her relief carefully controlled. "So David Foster is still here."

"Yeah, he's still here, and mad as hornets."

"He's the one we're here to see. It's important. Please, our talking to him might even help you with all this."

The officer looked newly interested. "What are you? Family?"

"Yes," Mary said simply.

"He told us he didn't have any family."

"He lied."

"Family feud?"

"You could say that."

The officer lowered his voice. "If you talk to him, you think he'll tell you anything? About that freak?"

"Maybe. How did he get out?"

"I told you—he just walked out. Right through the doors and the walls. We swiped at him but our hands went right through him. He got out of here and just went up in a pillar of fire—right there. You see the mark."

"I do," Mary said. She didn't bother to tell him they were hoping to walk David right out as well, if necessary.

"But it wasn't suicide or nothing. There's no body. He just disappeared. You ask me, the fire was just for show. Big bloody circus act." His face darkened. "You can lead us to him, I'll let you in. I want that freakazoid dead. He killed our men—murdered them in cold blood."

"That has to be proven, doesn't it?"

"He confessed it. Told us all about it. Had fun doing it." To her surprise, there were tears in the man's eyes. "Those were my pards. We went to academy together. We worked the streets together. If justice can't get to that guy, I don't want this badge anymore. I'll trade it in for something that doesn't kill me with how much I can't do anything."

"We want justice done too," Mary agreed. "We'll help you anyway we can. What's your name?"

"Captain Jeff Rogers."

"Jeff, if you'll let us talk to David, we'll do all we can to help you get to Clint. You're right—he's not dead. He's out there somewhere, and he will kill again if he's not stopped."

The officer stepped back and looked the four of them over, new light coming into his eyes.

"There's something different about you people."

"We can help," April cut in. "But we need you to help us first."

"It's possible," Mary said quietly, "that you might not like how we help at first. Something might happen . . . do you know what I'm saying?"

"Listen, lady, right now I don't care. You can break every law in the bloody book if you want to. I'll call it bail. Just get us to the freak."

Mary stuck out her hand, and they shook. "We'll do the best we can."

He looked around and gestured with his head. "Follow me."

The jail wasn't a large one. They passed through the office and into the secured area in the back, and David was there, glaring up at them from the corner of a cell. Mary recognized the woman who had been at the house—Jessica Parks—in another cell, but they were pointedly ignoring each other.

A third cell had been caution taped off. Its bars looked like something had melted through them.

Or someone.

"He's strong," Mary said, half to herself. "I've never seen one so strong."

"Because you've never seen power," David said. "You've gone your whole life with your eyes closed, denying that anything in this world can be stronger and truer than you are."

"There is nothing 'true' about the demons, David," Mary answered. "Or about those who allow them in."

"And you would know," David said. "From your vast experience being beaten by them."

"You're a very bitter man."

"And you're a very foolish woman."

They stared at each other for a few minutes. The others, clustered together behind Mary, shifted their feet and looked at one another, Rogers looked pointedly at Mary. "I'm going to step out for a minute," he said. "Stay put."

She nodded. "Thank you."

"So what?" David asked when Rogers had left. "You've all come as a small mob to do what? Kill me? I'm trapped here.

The only one with the power to get me out abandoned me here, just to show that he's stronger and smarter and that I need him. Idiot can't see the power in acting as one. So here you are. This is your chance."

"We don't want to kill you, David."

There. The words were out there. Implicit in them the suggestion that they would, if they had to.

He smirked. "Learning that not everything goes the way you want it to, are you?"

"Nothing ever has. I didn't want the massacre all those years ago. I didn't want to lose so many I cared about. I certainly didn't want to lose you."

"You say that like you knew. Like you had any idea how much it cost me. Like I haven't just been some nameless, face-less piece of the Oneness, hiding out in Lincoln where you never thought of or cared about me at all." He lifted his eyes and addressed the others. "This woman, she's your mother, isn't she? The matron of the village den, holding you all together and caring about everyone equally. The truth is she cares about no one equally. You're just cogs in a system. Like all the Oneness."

"No, David," Mary said, her whole voice a groan, a burden. "No, that's your hive."

"Then why didn't you know about me?" David asked. "Why is it that even now, you hardly remember me? Why is it that you have no idea what turned me, when you were there? You were right in the middle of it."

Her face paled.

This, she didn't know.

He had told her before that he blamed her for his pain because she had brought him into the Oneness.

And to her shame, she didn't really remember that. She had vague memories of David as a young man, years of vague awareness that he was leading the cell in Lincoln.

That was all.

He had not told her, before now, that she was also involved somehow in the very event that had turned him.

He settled back against the wall, clearly satisfied. "See, children? She doesn't even know what I'm talking about. That's how much she cares. That's how much Oneness binds people together, heart to heart, in love and unity. So much that she watched my life destroyed, and she doesn't even remember."

David was not a remarkable man to look at. Like so many of the Oneness, he would blend into any crowd. His hair, thinning in middle age, was cropped short. His face was a little heavyset but not fat, his build was average. His eyes were creased with laugh lines, and his face still, despite how twisted they had seen it, despite all the bitterness coming out his mouth, looked kind. He wore his own clothes in the cell, just jeans and a polo shirt. He was just a man, a brother, like any of them.

"I don't know what to say," Mary said. "It's true. I don't remember. Tell me the story, and give me a chance to put the pieces together."

"No, I don't think so," he said, enjoying himself. "I don't think so. I think I want to wait and see if you ever recall it on your own."

"David, whatever happened, I am sorry. I would apologize— would try to make things right. But I can't do that in the dark."

"Seems to me the dark is your natural habitat. I'm just doing all I can to make you see that."

He closed his eyes for a nanosecond, during which they could see him processing something—they didn't know what. And he opened them again.

"So have you come to kill me, or what?"

"No. We're here to talk to you."

He laughed. "That's classic. Why don't you do the thing right? Really get into cahoots with your police buddies and spirit me off somewhere with no address. Torture me until I tell you all. Until I reveal how vast and nefarious my plan really is, and how doomed to failure you already are."

"That's not the kind of talk we want to have."

"But you will if you have to, right? Your black friend will tie me up and play cattle drive with a taser until I give in screaming."

"Mary," April said sharply. "Don't let him get to you."

"Oh, I'll get to you," David said. His eyes gleamed. "As long as you insist on 'talking to me,' I'll get to you. As long as you make me stay here, here on this planet as part of the Oneness, I'll get to you."

Mary sighed. She opened her mouth to answer but stopped herself short and turned around, doing a 180 to face Chris and April.

"I can't do this."

"You . . ." April felt her way forward. "What can't you do?"

"I can't talk to him. Not in here. Not like this. We need to get him out of here."

Chris lifted an eyebrow and hid a smile. "Somewhere with no address?"

"That's not funny, Chris."

His eyebrows went back to normal. "No, it's not. But I'm going to enjoy the picture he was painting for just a minute anyway." Chris strode forward and grabbed the cell bars, his fingers straining around the cast on his arm, standing over David like Atlas over some mere man. "Listen, weasel. As sick as you are, you are still Oneness, and they love you. I do not. You can joke all you want about turning them in ways you know they will never be turned, but you do not know me or what I will do. Behave yourself. You understand me? We're going to get you out of here, like you said, and go somewhere with no address, and you are going to talk to the ladies like they want to talk. If I catch you threatening them, if I catch you making their lives any harder than you've already made them, in ways that are unnecessary, I might just throw you overboard." He smiled grimly. "Literally. Got that?"

David cocked his head. "Is that supposed to scare me? You should have figured something out by now, boy. I want to die. I want to be released."

"But you can't," April said slowly. "That's the missing piece of all this. You can't even commit suicide, because even after death you would still be Oneness. You're really trying to get us to destroy you somehow. To really and truly disconnect you."

His smile was thin, letting something else show through other than the mockery and hatred they were becoming accustomed to. Exhaustion, bitter weariness. "You're clever."

"I don't think we can do that," April said.

"So I'm told. But I don't give up hope."

April put an arm around Mary and hugged her tightly. She blew out a breath of air, shaking her head as her eyes stayed on David. "What are we getting into?"

David opened his mouth to offer his own answer to that question, but Chris saw the movement and barked out, "Shut it."

David obeyed.

His eyes were still gleaming.

Like the proverbial cat that swallowed the canary.

This was their offensive. Their jump on him. So why did they feel like they had walked into another trap?

**The air on the way** to Tempter's Mountain grew stiffer and dustier as they turned on the dirt roads up the mountain. Susan Brown followed Richard—with the children, Dr. Smith, and Angelica in his car—in a sandy-coloured, nondescript fifteen-passenger van. All the house kids were in there, along with Tony and Dr. Smith's family.

And the closer they got to the hermit's old hideaway, the easier Richard could breathe.

Past scrub and pines, he made a hard left to get around a small gully in the road. Taxpayer money didn't exactly go toward the roads up here. A quick check in his rearview showed Susan keeping up admirably, with half a dozen heads bounding gamely behind her.

He smiled.

"What's funny?" Jordan asked.

There was a little desperation in the question. Richard looked down at him for half a second, then back to the road and hard right around another pothole. "Watching all the heads in Miss Brown's van bounce."

"Why do we have to come up here anyway?" Jordan said, apparently not seeing the humour. "It's so far. And I hate the country."

"Because it's safe," Richard answered. "You know you're not safe right now. The demons will come after you again. So will the hive. They've got Alex, and they knew exactly where you were. You'll be safer up here."

"Don't know why," Jordan said, folding his arms. He was sitting in the passenger seat beside Richard, and his legs just touched the floor. He was small for his age, short and scrawny. Hard to believe he'd been a dangerous enemy only a little while ago.

But demons didn't much care about age or size. All they wanted was someone they could control and fascinate.

The fascination was even worse than the control. Control, everyone would sooner or later want to break free from. But the fascination would draw them back.

Hardly conscious he was doing it, Richard prayed silently. Spirit, draw them. Draw them in. Join them.

Don't let these little ones go back.

"You know how powerful witchcraft made Clint," Richard said.

"Yeah."

"Well, in the Oneness we have power too. A very different kind, but real power. The man who lived up here used it. He built a shield over the whole property, especially the house. The demons can't operate under it."

"The hive could still come."

"Yes, but the human part of the hive isn't as hard to fight."

"That's why Charlie died," Alicia said, chiming in from the backseat. "Alex told us."

Richard frowned. "Who is Charlie?"

"Your friend killed him. Alex said it was under a shield."

So the fake Dr. Smith had a name.

Of course he did, Richard chided himself. He was human too.

Had been human too.

In his case, the shield that disarmed the demon was one of Richard's making. He had not built it purposely. In all their years in the fishing village, the little cell never really expected to be attacked. But Richard's habit of concentrated, protracted prayer—immersion in the Spirit, participation in the pulsing veins of all that truly was—had made the cell house a place where demons could not abide. Could not manifest. Could not control.

If he had created the shield on purpose, it would not have been with the intent of making hive members more killable. No more than April had killed the man—Charlie? he tried the name on like it was an old shoe that was too warped to fit comfortably—intentionally. She hadn't really talked about it, but Shelley told the story, over and over, wide-eyed, and Diane echoed it. The man had died because he held on. Because he wasn't willing to let the demons go.

Because like so much of mankind, he was passionately committed to his own destruction.

They turned up one more dirt road, bounced up a steep incline, and they were there.

The little house sat nestled against an embankment. Knotty pines and scrub surrounded it; the yard was just dirt and sand and stones. Weeds had sprouted and grown along the walkway. Other than that, it did not look like anything had changed.

Richard turned his car off and just sat while Susan pulled the van beside him. The hermitage was going to be a tight squeeze for this whole crew, but coming here had been right—right and necessary. He could feel the difference, the presence of the shield, the presence of—

He stopped.

He wasn't sure what that presence was.

Slowly, he got out of the car, into the beating sun. Its heat glared down and then bounced back up from the barren ground, engulfing him. The air smelled like hot rock and pine. It was a scent he remembered well. It had been summer, like this, when he first came and sought out the hermit and learned from him more about how to pray.

He had been here twice since. Once with Reese and Mary and the boys, when Reese was badly wounded from a demon attack and still under the illusion of exile. And the hermit had thought her an enemy and reproached Richard for bringing her here, but had sheltered them anyway and had given his life when David found them and shot the old man, not under the influence of any demon that could be stopped by the shield, but in his own cold blood.

The second time when he came back here, after all that was over, to bury his old friend.

They had debated telling the authorities. Calling a morgue. Filing a charge of murder. They hadn't done it. The old man lived off the grid up here, out of the eye of the world, and he died the same way. Richard thought he would want it that way. He had come back and buried the body behind the house.

He had lamented.

But he smiled now. He almost wanted to laugh. Because the first two times he had come here, he had felt the hermit's presence like a tangible thing, like the old man liked to go invisible and hang around and look over their shoulders as they came up the drive. His spirit was strong—pungent—like that.

And now Richard felt it that way again.

Like the man had never died.

As truly he hadn't.

Oneness, more than the sum of its parts, was life. You could not lose that just because your body ceased to breathe and create new cells and pump blood.

Doors slammed as Susan and the house kids and Dr. Smith's family got out of the van and stood in the dirt, looking around, most of them skeptically. Richard supposed this bunch of city kids mostly felt like Jordan did about the country. Jordan himself was stubbornly staying in the car, breathing in every last breath of air-conditioned air before someone made him get out in the heat.

Angelica climbed out, said something polite to Dr. Smith, and then stood next to Richard.

"It's like he's still here," she said. "Like I can still feel him here."

"I think he is," Richard said.

"In the cloud?"

"Yes."

And then he laughed. Out loud, with surprise and delight. Because for one split second, standing and smiling at him from the front step of the house, he saw a woman with long dark hair and a simple white dress.

Then she was gone.

But not gone.

"I don't think he's the only one," Richard said, grinning at Angelica. "Did you see her?"

"Her?"

"Never mind. This is good . . . it's good we're here. You and Tony can keep this whole bunch safe here. You'll have help."

"So you're not staying?" Angelica said, watching as the house kids milled around and Alicia and Jordan finally emerged from the rental car.

"I have to follow a lead," he said. "They haven't given me much, but enough to go after for now."

"Do you think we're going to be attacked?"

"Something will happen. The hive may not know where we are—they won't find you here easily. But they will want the children back."

He dropped his voice so no one else could hear it. "Keep

a close eye on them. Jordan especially, but both of them. And pray they Join the Oneness."

She looked at them, then at Richard, concerned. "What are you worried about?"

"It's not that easy to leave demonic possession, even if you wanted out. It's like an addiction. You may hate yourself for it, but you'll keep going back."

Sorrow flashed across her face. "Oh, but they wouldn't. They're just kids. They wouldn't . . ."

"They already do. Jordan already misses it. They weren't 'just kids' when they were possessed. They were powerful. Something special. And they knew it. Watch them."

She nodded. "Yes, sir."

"Tell Tony."

"I will."

Dr. Smith was standing just a little apart with his wife, Valerie, by his side. Richard stepped back and nodded, raising his voice as he called out to him. "Well, this is it. Home sweet home."

"There's not much room, is there?" Valerie asked.

"Unfortunately not." Richard drew closer to them so he could talk without all the house kids overhearing. "But that might make it easier to keep an eye on everyone. The shield—the protection over this place—extends a ways. They can explore the cliffs, even go down to the bay if they want to. Keep the new ones closer than that—almost housebound. They won't like it, but it's necessary."

Dr. Smith nodded and didn't ask why. Richard continued, "Jordan tells me he hates the country anyway, so hopefully you can find a TV or something inside and keep him occupied. The more occupied the better."

"Who was the man who lived here?" Dr. Smith asked.

Richard paused, not entirely sure how to answer that. "A friend. A brother. He was a hermit—a contemplative, if you want. Spent his life thinking and praying."

"Not a way to make a living," Valerie observed.

Richard smiled. "He didn't eat much."

He hesitated, then chuckled to himself. "Dr. and Mrs. Smith, do you believe in ghosts?"

"I don't know," Valerie answered. "Why?"

"Well, I don't. But we in the Oneness, we go on . . . the connection holds after death. Life doesn't end. We call those on the other side the cloud. They are not ghosts like you understand them."

"Why are you telling us this?" Dr. Smith asked.

"Because they're here," Richard said. "At least two of them, I think."

Valerie blanched just a little, and Dr. Smith looked intrigued. "Are we likely to see them?" she asked.

"No, no. I don't know that non-Oneness can see the cloud. But I thought you'd like to know you're not alone, and it's not just the twins watching out for you."

He didn't know if they were aware how much he was giving an invitation.

It was the old benediction of the Oneness, the watchword that gave meaning to their whole lives:

Not alone.

Never alone.

Never, ever alone.

**While Lieutenant Jackson worked** on the necessary paperwork to get Jacob released into Reese's custody, she left Tyler to wait there and drove a few doors down to a safe house where witnesses sometimes were given a place.

Jackson had told her about it and said that Miranda and her mother were there, and that Miranda had been asking about her.

Reese's heart was heavy as she pulled into the driveway and rang the bell, heavy as the door was opened and she explained who she was, heavy as she was ushered into the living room and asked to wait while the girl and her mother were called.

But the expression on Miranda's face when she rushed into the room was nothing but relief.

"Oh, I'm so glad you're all right!" she cried. To Reese's shock, she threw herself across the room and into a tight, childlike hug, nearly knocking her backwards on her crutches. "When you left and I realized you were going after Clint, I was so worried," she babbled. "I wished I hadn't told you anything about him. But did you find your friends? Is everything okay?"

Reese needed a moment to process the questions, and to process Miranda herself—she had expected a broken, basket case of a girl. It struck her that even after everything that had happened, Miranda remained so innocent and so naive that she did not even realize how serious everything was.

She didn't know to be more preoccupied by her own problems than enthralled by Reese's.

Because that's what she was—enthralled. She tugged at Reese's arm as she pulled out of the hug, urging her to sit down beside her on the couch. "Tell me everything that happened. Where did you go? Was Clint there? Was Tyler hurt? Was . . "

"Miranda." The voice, weary, cut her off. "Give Reese a minute to think."

Reese lifted her eyes to the living room doorway, where Miranda's mother, Julie stood.

And there was the broken basket case Reese had expected. Her eyes were swollen and red. She looked like she hadn't slept in days.

She looked like she had aged.

Miranda was back to prattling something, and Reese realized she had tuned her out. "Oh, I'm sorry . . . Miranda, hold on a moment."

She released herself from the girl's hold, stood, and approached Julie slowly.

"It's awful, what's happened," Reese said. "But it's going to be okay."

"We killed a man," Julie said. Her eyes flicked across Reese's shoulder. "My daughter . . ."

Reese turned, taking over, knowing it meant something to Julie to not be the one giving orders. "Miranda, can you give us a few minutes alone?"

The girl's lip jutted out in an immediate pout, but with an expression of guilt over her own reaction, the girl nodded and left. She slowed a moment as she passed them both in the doorway, but a firm nod from Reese sent her the rest of the way out.

The moment she was gone, Julie began to cry.

This time it was Reese squeezing Julie's arm awkwardly around the crutch, leading her to the couch, sitting her down, and embracing her like a sister.

"It's okay," she murmured.

Julie did not try to pull away, and Reese did not let go. She felt movement through her arms, through her embrace, a great drawing force, a presence far more than herself.

She was not just one woman offering solidarity.

She was the Oneness offering life and community forever amen.

Julie looked into her eyes and said, "Yes, I want to be what you are."

And they both closed their eyes and felt it. Julie gasped.

The change.

The Joining.

Their spirits surged into one another and became one, and

surged into the Other, and the others, and became one; their worlds expanded, joined, contracted, embraced.

Neither of them spoke.

They didn't have to.

Their souls knew each other.

It was the first time Reese had truly felt One since the exile.

They really didn't know how much time passed before Julie said, "Why did Jacob try to keep this from us? I know he is one of you."

"One of us."

She smiled. "One of us."

"I don't know. I don't know much about him. But we've come to take him away. He needs to face what he is—and what we are. He needs the truth."

"Yes," Julie said, her eyes filling with tears. "Can you show him? Can you help him? I know . . . I know what he did was wrong, so wrong."

"Do you know what happened to him?" Reese asked. "Did he ever tell you—why he feels the way he does about the Oneness?"

"Why he thinks you're all infidels?"

"Yes. Thanks for putting that so kindly."

Julie wrinkled her nose. "He's called you a lot worse." She thought about it a moment. "No, he's never told us exactly what sparked it. But he tells us about what Oneness is supposed to be, and he tells us stories of its failures and how—excuse me— perverted it has become."

Reese sighed. "I don't think you need to pass those stories on. I think we're going to hear them for ourselves."

Julie looked anxious. "Are you going to visit him?"

"More than that. He's coming away with us. He agreed to it—to travel with us and question himself."

"He'll try to teach you," Julie said, alarmed, "and turn you to his way of thinking. He's so convincing."

"We know. That was part of our agreement." Reese laughed, even though she felt nervous about the idea herself. "Don't look so worried. We aren't going to be that easily swayed."

"You haven't spent time with Jacob before."

"I know he's gifted. But I've been in this fight too long, and too hard, to let anyone convince me that what's wrong is right. Or that demons are the real power of God in this world."

Julie's face darkened. "He wasn't always that far gone. At first, when we first started following him, there were no demons. That didn't change until Clint came."

"Is that when you started to question him?"

Julie blanched a little. "How did you know I was?"

"Miranda told me that Jacob wanted her to marry Clint. You're her mother. I can't see you—"

"It was wrong!" Julie burst out, her eyes full of tears. "They all told me I was being unreasonable. And I didn't protest in front of Miranda—I didn't want to encourage her to rebel. She did that on her own."

"Would you have let it go through?" Reese asked. "If Miranda hadn't decided for herself that she was afraid of him—if everything hadn't gone down the way it did—"

"I hope not. I hope I would have left. Would have taken her away."

"But you don't know."

"No, I don't know. Everything seems so clear out here—but then . . ."

"I understand," Reese said. "When you're being deceived—it's a strong thing, a lie."

"Very strong." Julie looked away, ashamed of herself. Reese wanted to keep talking to her, to tell her it wasn't her fault and she had nothing to be ashamed of. But she couldn't. This one, Julie had to work through for herself. They were silent for a few minutes, and Julie gave way to a small smile. She laid her hand on Reese's hand. "But I am Oneness now," she said. "Truly."

"Yes, you are."

"So how can I help? You're fighting a battle. Can I fight it too?"

"Yes," Reese said, "you can."

"How?"

"Pray."

"I don't think I know how."

"You'll learn. Ask the Spirit to teach you. He will. You're Oneness—prayer is like breathing. Or dreaming. You'll learn."

"I will," Julie agreed softly. "Is there anything else?"

"Just keep seeking out the truth," Reese said. "The more free you are, the more free we all are."

"I think I can do that."

Reese smiled. "I know you can."

* * * *

The heat wavering off the blacktop when Reese returned to
the correctional facility made her head swim. Tyler was waiting on the sidewalk in front of the building with a tall man
standing next to him, clutching a bag. Jacob. She couldn't see
him clearly at first, but she knew who he was from the fist in
her stomach.

He looked at her reproachfully when she walked up to them.
His dark, stern eyes looked right through her—he knew. And
she felt guilt.

For bringing Julie into the Oneness.

"They are my family," Jacob said quietly. "And you have been
spreading rumours about me, slandering me to them behind
my back."

"No rumours necessary," Reese said, the fist in her stomach
tightening. "They've seen for themselves the reality of what you
are and what you've taught them."

"You think I'm a deceiver."

"I think you're deceived."

"So," he asked, still clutching the paper bag that Reese
assumed held the few personal effects he'd brought with him,
"who first? Do I try to convince you, or do you try to convince
me?"

"We're first," Reese said. "This is our offensive."

"Fair enough," was all he said, but he let his eyes flicker to Tyler for a moment and rest there reproachfully as well, as though to say, "Do you always let her tell you what to do?"

Tyler shot Reese a look but didn't respond to either of them.

Jacob started talking again when they were only halfway across the parking lot to the car, his voice booming even though he was trying to be quiet. "So, let us make our objectives clear. You are going to try to teach me the error of my ways and convert me back to a more worldly understanding of the Oneness. To cause me to repent my ways."

"More or less, yes," Reese said. "Actually, I just want you to see the truth."

"And in turn I am going to show you what the Oneness truly is. I'm going to show you that you are deceived, that you've been living all your lives in a half-truth. And when we're done all this, I hope that you, my sister and my brother, will join me in leading the Oneness back to purity and power."

Reese didn't answer.

He was so sincere.

Not even just about his twisted point of view and his desire to prove his points. He actually cared about her. And Tyler. And thought he was doing right by them.

They got into the car, and Jacob seated himself without asking in the front seat, bumping Tyler to the back. Reese slid into the driver's seat next to him, not happy with the idea of Tyler driving up front alone with this man. Yes, she would be in the backseat, but still . . .

As she started the car, Jacob asked, "Well, then, you may as well begin. Where are you taking me, and what do you hope I will learn from it?"

"Remember your end of the bargain," Reese said, looking over her shoulder as she backed the car out of their parking spot. "You will question yourself."

Jacob had the audacity to laugh. "You seem to think that makes me vulnerable. As though I've never questioned myself all these years—as though I haven't asked question after question. But yes, I'll remember my end."

"Good," Reese said. She eased the car onto the road and headed for the highway.

She hated to do this to Tyler.

But it was the place where Jacob's questioning needed to begin.

"Are you going to explain?" he asked again, several minutes after they had merged into traffic.

"No," Reese said. "Not until we get there."

"Seems a shame to waste this time," Jacob said, shifting his weight back to give more room to long legs and reclining in comfort as though he was completely at home. And in charge. "No speeches, no thoughts you want me to chew on."

"Okay, sure," Reese said. "You know what happened with Julie. You felt it."

"Of course I did. I've been living at close quarters with Julie for years. She had almost come into your Oneness many times, and I've stepped in to prevent it. I knew the instant you brought her over."

"I didn't," Reese said. "She crossed on her own. She answered the call of the Spirit, like she's been trying to do for years."

"So." Jacob said. "Yes, I knew. What do you want me to gather from that?"

Reese held her temper at his tone. Somehow his playing humble student made his arrogance that much harder to handle.

"If the Oneness as we know it is all a sham, like you say, then why does it work? Why do you know the instant someone becomes One? Why do you feel me to be a sister, like I know you to be a brother, if we're just a twisted perversion of what the Oneness is meant to be?"

"I never said that you are not Oneness," Jacob said. "You are. Truly."

"Then what . . ."

"But the Oneness has been corrupted. You have accepted false practices and false beliefs, and they've weakened and infected everything, so much so that you cannot tell truth from lie or power from weakness. The call to be One is a call to power and to purity, and you have neither. Yes, you have unity. But you do not remember what that unity is for."

Tyler made a noise in the backseat, but he kept quiet. Reese pulled onto the highway and wondered if he knew where she was going.

"Our unity holds the world together," Reese said. "It's the fabric keeping everything from tearing apart. In the Spirit."

"Talk," Jacob said. "You use those words, but you don't even understand what they mean. You don't have any concept of how the world is fraying or what you need to do to keep it from reeling into total chaos. Yes, you exist to hold the world together. But you're not doing it. You think you can accomplish the work of the Oneness just by patting each other on the back, and holding prayer meetings, and serving people. You've lost your reason for being here."

Reese didn't really know what to say. The heat outside was making her ill. Or else Jacob's nearness, and his forceful conviction was. She set her jaw and kept driving, letting her speed inch up as she passed traffic and kept going toward the place.

She glanced in the rearview mirror and saw that Tyler had gone pale.

He knew, then.

I'm sorry, she thought in his direction. Oneness couldn't read each other's minds. But she hoped he could understand her heart.

Jacob stopped talking, thankfully, but she could feel him smouldering beside her. His presence was a force—like a storm front. Like a great mass pulling off the gravity of everything and everyone around him.

She did have to admit that he had power. More than your average member of the Oneness. She didn't know exactly what it looked like, or how it manifested other than in a lot of talk, but she knew he had it. It exuded from him. Electricity building up in storm clouds.

They reached the place, and Tyler got paler in the rearview mirror, and Jacob looked first surprised and then smug—even more smug and arrogant than he had the rest of the drive so far. She pulled off the side of the highway, grateful there wasn't much traffic.

Coming from Lincoln, the two directions of the highway had been separated by a grassy median. On the other side, the side heading for the city, both lanes had been blocked off by orange cones and caution tape, and traffic was routed over the median and onto the side where Reese had pulled off, narrowed to one lane in each direction. They got out of the car into the stifling heat, and Reese saw Tyler shiver like he was cold.

"I'm sorry," she said.

I know," he said.

"I thought it was necessary."

"It probably is."

They looked both ways, waited for a couple of cars to pass going toward the city, and then crossed the lanes and the median. The grass was dry like straw, and they disturbed a cloud of insects. Reese waved them away and led onward, stalwart, toward the place where Clint had murdered two policemen who had pulled him over. With Tyler and Chris in the truck. Sent from Jacob's farm.

They could still see blood on the asphalt and on the mile marker and the rail beside the road.

Tyler blanched. Reese thought he might be sick then and there. All colour had drained from his face, and he stared at the place, at the ground, at the memory.

"Did you see it?" Jacob asked. Clearly he knew what had happened here.

"No," Tyler said. "I heard it. I was inside—I couldn't see. And I didn't look."

"I'm sorry," Reese said again, very quietly.

She was. She didn't, really didn't, want to put him through this.

"Why are we here?" Jacob asked. No making bones, this one.

"The awful thing," Reese said, "the really awful thing, is that to some degree you, who are our brother and are supposed to serve the Spirit, are responsible for this. Men died here. Innocent men."

But Jacob shook his head. "There is no such thing as an innocent man."

"Are you saying they deserved to die?"

"Clint acts in the power of God," Jacob said. "You want to know what threatens to tear the world apart? Injustice. Sin. That men are allowed to get away with very murder, when they wear a badge. And no one even knows. But Clint does. He is animated by the Spirit of God to bring justice. As he did here."

She stared at him. He was looking around, seeing the blood, imagining the carnage, and his face was totally impassive. If anything, he looked satisfied.

She wanted to be sick, and not because of the murders.

Reese had seen a lot of terrible things in her years of demon hunting. More than Tyler could imagine, really. Nothing quite so horrifying as what he had been party to here, but plenty to turn her stomach.

But Jacob's stomach wasn't turned. He was nodding, slowly.

"What do you think they did to deserve this?" Reese asked.

He just looked at her, giving no answer.

The reality was slowly dawning on her. "You think this is

what the Oneness is supposed to do? Kill people?"

"Restore justice. Restore order. You said it yourself: we are threatened with chaos. We are threatened with the wrongs men do, the things we call sin and evil. If those things are not corrected, if they are not paid for—yes, sometimes even in blood—then we will lose the world. It will descend into darkness."

He met her eyes forcefully, his own burning like lamps in a dark face. "You want to do the right thing, Reese. But you, and all who are like you, are doing it the wrong way. You are contributing to the problem, not helping to solve it. Purity and power. We have to come back to our roots—to our reason for being."

"Not this!" Tyler said. His voice was high, barely controlled. He stood on the asphalt, surrounded by orange cones and yellow tape, and spread his arms and circled slowly around. "Not this! This isn't what we're here to do. This is what we're here to fight. What Clint did was wrong—it was evil. He killed innocent men!"

"I told you," Jacob answered. "There are no innocent men."

He advanced, almost as though he would swing a fist and knock Tyler for a loop, but instead he put his arm around him. Tyler pulled aside, a look of revulsion on his face, but Jacob's own face was burning with passion now, white and earnest. "Do you want to know what those men had done? Then I challenge you to find out the truth. Do you know how many criminals hide behind badges? How many law enforcement officers do everything but? The fact that you are working with the police in all of this only goes to show how far gone you are—how far from the purity of the Oneness you've come. I have rescued girls from being trafficked by the very men whose deaths you're

mourning. I've stopped drug deals while the police were looking the other way, with their pockets padded for it. Greed and
injustice—that's all that's driving them. Killed innocent men?
Oh no. Clint—or rather, the Spirit that works in him—only
put something right here. He mended what was tearing in the
fabric of the world, as you put it, Reese. He did what none of
you were willing to do, what none of you have the courage or
the conviction to do. You are all too compromised, too weak."

"You do keep telling us that," Reese said. She felt sick. Not
only because Jacob was so unmovable, but because he was right.

Or at least, too close to right for her comfort.

He wasn't the only one who had seen police aiding the
crimes they were supposed to stop. He wasn't the only one who
had seen men whose job it was to hold up the torch of law and
order contributing to the darkness instead.

But she had never fought the men. Only the demons. They
had tried to help influence arrests or get innocent people out of
trouble, but she'd never believed the battle was primarily fought
on a human front. Yes, the Spirit called people. And the Oneness sometimes rescued them. But they didn't set out to bring
justice or attack those who were serving and working alongside
the demonic.

And now, even though she was certain that Clint was not
anything good, that he was as opposed to the goals of the Oneness as it was possible to be, she wondered if Jacob could be
right, at all, in theory.

And with that moment of wondering, her mind was off,
travelling the trails of her memory, reconfiguring every fight,
every event. What could have been different if they had taken

the people out. It was rare that they ever fought a core, like they had at the warehouse: a gathering of demons, disembodied, empowered by a single great evil. Almost always, the fights were around people: possessed, oppressed, or just following their own lusts and greed with the help of the darkness. And if they had attacked them.

If they had gone after the people, the tools.

If they had stopped Clint long before he became what he was now.

If they had gotten to the men who were used in the massacre twenty years ago, the one that had killed Chris's father and so many others.

If they had identified David.

And stopped him.

Before the exile.

"Reese?" Tyler asked. He had come up beside her, and his voice was quiet, gentle, pressing. "Are you okay?"

She shook her head. "Yeah. I'm fine."

"Is something wrong?"

"No." She looked away from him, and her eyes met Jacob's. He was watching her intently, and he nodded, slightly, and his voice softened.

"I know that what happened here was awful," he said. "It's hard to see how it could have been for the good. But I am telling you, it was. Take me up on my challenge. Look into the histories of the men who were killed here, if you can even get access to them. I didn't understand why Clint had done it when I first heard the news. I'll admit it bothered me. But when I heard their names—at least one of these men has a history worse than you can imagine."

His eyes intensified, as though he knew he had her.

"In fact, one of these men, one of the 'innocent' men killed here, was central to what happened twenty years ago."

Her knees felt weak.

The sun was calling up mirages from the highway on every side, wavering the world in its reverse rays.

"You know what I'm talking about," he said.

"Were you there? Is that what happened to you—to start you on this road?"

"Oh yes, I was there. I lost everything. But I'm not like your David. I didn't lose faith in the Oneness. I just realized the Oneness wasn't doing what it was supposed to do. We never should have been vulnerable like we were. We never should have lost people, never should have gone down when the demons attacked."

"I thought you said the demons were on our side."

"No, I said Clint is on our side. The demonic is just a source of power. He's learned how to use it. You know as well as I do what demons on their own are. Scattered, frantic, purposeless. They just destroy. We're meant to get them under control."

"We're meant to battle them," Reese insisted, her tone more vehement than she felt. "We're meant to be the other side. To hold together what they are trying to tear apart."

To her surprise, he just shrugged. "Have it your own way,"

he said. He turned and gazed down the highway, into the heat, beyond the blockade. And she saw him for a moment as he saw himself: the lone voice in the wilderness, one strong man who believed in the truth and stood for it against all others, even against those who thought they were doing right, but were deceived. Even against her.

"We should go, Reese."

She turned back to look at Tyler. His expression was haggard. Sweat was trickling down his face, but not just from the sun. He looked concerned, and afraid, and sick.

"You can't tell me what happened here wasn't evil," he said.

Then he turned on Jacob. "It didn't end here, you know. Your hero, this Clint guy, he didn't just kill the policemen. Maybe that was justified—maybe you're right, and he knew things I didn't. But you can't tell me he was good or right in the way he did it, because I heard—I heard him . . ." He stopped and shuddered, and didn't finish the thought. Didn't put words to the memory. "But he didn't stop here. He took me and Chris to a house where he tried to kill us both. What did we do, Jacob? What evils are lurking in our past?" The words should have been fired at the man, a volley of passionate defence. But they weren't. Tyler sounded tired, and like he was really asking.

Like he thought it was possible they deserved to die somehow.

Jacob just looked at him and said, "But you're not dead."

"Because Reese and the others intervened. And the strength of the Oneness came through for me."

The big man shrugged, a tiny smile playing behind his

beard. "Maybe. Or maybe everything happened exactly how it was supposed to all along. Maybe you needed to come back to me, like you are now, open and ready to listen. At the farm, you were closed. Your friend was addling your brain. You had too many suspicions, too many—"

Tyler interrupted, and this time the heat was there. "Don't you blame anything on Chris."

"He isn't Oneness," Jacob said. And his eyes strayed to Reese, and she thought he was looking through her. "You're both taking direction and partnership from someone who refuses to become One. What does that say about you? Or about him?"

Reese flushed and turned back to the car. "Let's go."

"You've seen all you want me to see here?"

"Yes."

"Not very impressive, I'm afraid."

She didn't know how the man could be so infuriating and so convincing at the same time. How he could inspire her to think new thoughts, and question her whole existence, and at the same time make her want to punch him in the face.

Of course, it didn't help that he had brought up Chris.

She didn't want to think about Chris right now.

They got back into the car, and she jacked up the air conditioning and was frustrated that it barely responded. The air blew warm. She put the car in gear and backed out onto the highway, glad again that there was no traffic for the moment. She wasn't sure she would have processed the presence of other cars properly—her mind was spinning.

At least she understood better how a whole community of people could have followed Jacob so blindly.

Julie's conversion came back to her and strengthened her, like a hug or a warm message. She had lived with this man and come to believe that he was wrong. She had been hurt by him. Her daughter had been hurt by him. He was dangerous.

"My turn," he said.

It took her a minute to process. "What?"

"It's my turn. You said we would trade. You lead and I follow. I followed you here. I considered what you said."

Tyler made another sound from the backseat, but Reese ignored it.

Despite Jacob's insistence on the highway of his own rightness, she believed him. He had, to some degree, considered their side.

And she was keeping her end of the bargain and considering his.

Calmly, naturally, he told her where to go. Where to switch highways, when to change lanes. Traffic grew heavier as they neared the city. In spite of herself, she was grateful for his guidance. She knew she should resent his taking her in hand, but she didn't. She was glad for it. Glad he was leading, because it gave her time to think.

To remind herself of what she knew was true.

Behind her, Tyler brooded.

They were silent, the only sound that of the a/c toiling and the engine growling as they drove. She knew Jacob wanted her to ask. About twenty years ago. About the dead policeman's role in what had happened. About Jacob's role in what happened.

Twenty years ago.

A dark, mostly undefined shadow that had lain at the back of Reese's whole life as Oneness. She had been only a child, and not One yet. By the time she came to Lincoln and became part of the cell there, twenty years ago was already a blot on the past that most people did not talk about. Especially David.

The cell would sometimes refer to it, whispering things, especially when David seemed morose or angry, which he did—maybe more often than most. Looking back, it was impossible to tell whether the signs of his disillusionment and enmity had been there all along, mistaken for normal discouragement and irritation.

After the last few months, Reese was disinclined to trust any impression as true, past or present.

But she had known, always, that something had happened twenty years ago. An attack, they said. A massacre, when they were more specific. There had been bombings, and killings after that, and Oneness on the road as fugitives. And the police had been involved somehow—not on their side, like they were now.

Assuming of course, that Lieutenant Jackson and the rest of the department that was letting him get away with working with the Oneness really were on their side.

And when Reese moved to the village cell, after her exile, after Chris and Tyler and Richard and Mary were the only people in the world who believed in her, she had learned that twenty years ago meant something to them too. Chris's father had been murdered twenty years ago. Mary had gone through whatever exactly it was that had happened.

She knew Jacob wanted her to ask.

She knew she needed to know. To learn more, because the past wasn't just in the past; it was influencing—even dictating—the present.

But she didn't open her mouth.

She didn't give him the gratification of knowing how much he had pulled her in.

And anyway.

She wasn't sure she was ready to face the past just yet.

**On Tempter's Mountain,** Tony kept a close eye on the boy, Jordan. He had not shared Angelica's dismayed protest over the idea that these kids could come back under the sway of the demons—could actually welcome them back. Not at all. Maybe because he wasn't a girl. Maybe because he was more driven, more punch-happy than Angelica had ever been. But he remembered how he had felt as a young boy when the Spirit first started to draw him, when he became One and then he learned he had the gift of swordsmanship and he became a hunter and a fighter, tracking down the demons and sending them howling into the night—or losing, sometimes. He remembered how it had shaped him. How it had made him. And he knew the demons had done the same for Jordan.

He knew Jordan was lost now without them.

He chewed a wad of gum and sat on the arm of the couch in the hermit's tiny living room, watching Jordan watch TV. They had dug the set out of a closet. It was ancient, its picture lined and crackling with static, its sound warped. Jordan had tuned out the old sitcom reruns in front of him twenty minutes ago.

He was just staring, blank-faced.

Thinking, Tony figured.

Richard had told him to keep the kids inside, especially Jordan. Stick him in front of the TV, dig out a Nintendo set if at all possible, occupy his brain and keep him from getting out from under the shield, or even out toward the periphery where the shield would be weaker.

But Tony didn't think just letting the kid zone out like this was a good idea.

He remembered that too—restlessness. Boredom. The kind of trouble it got him into as a kid.

Heck, he still got in trouble when he got bored.

He stood up and switched off the TV, waiting for Jordan to yell in protest.

He didn't.

Yup, this was bad.

"Come on," Tony said, "let's go hiking."

"You're not supposed to take me away from here," Jordan said.

He didn't know the kid had actually heard that.

"What are you talking about? It's just a hike. Come on."

"You're not supposed to let me out of the house." Jordan's eyes gleamed. "I'm too dangerous."

"No," Tony corrected him, "you're not. It's the demons that

are dangerous. I'm not supposed to get you away from the shield. But we can hike and stay under the shield. Come on, let's go."

Jordan folded his arms and sat back deeper in the springy, threadbare love seat that was the only place to sit in the room. "It's too hot."

"It's not so bad up here. It's cooler in the mountains, and there's a breeze off the water."

He slumped even farther. "I don't want to."

"Don't you like to go outside?"

"No, I hate it. I want to sit here and watch TV."

"You weren't watching TV," Tony pointed out in exasperation. "You were sitting there zoned out."

Jordan looked right at him. "Does that scare you?"

Tony knelt right in front of him and said, "Stop it. Right now."

"Stop what?"

"What you're doing. Playing with the idea of going back. Pretending you're still possessed and I'm supposed to be scared of you."

"You are scared of me," Jordan said, very quietly.

"Kid, this is not a game."

"I know that."

Tony looked into the boy's eyes and tried to search them. He had never been a deep one—never been the type of Oneness that drew people and connected deeply with them, that saw destiny in others and tried to call it forth. That was the kind of thing

Richard and people like him did. Not kids, sword-swinging teenagers, like Tony.

But he needed to get through to this boy.

Because he knew, as he looked into Jordan's eyes, that either one day this child would fight alongside him, closer than a brother, or else they would battle one another to the death.

"Let's go for a walk," Tony insisted.

Jordan huffed and threw himself off the couch, scowling. "Fine."

Despite Tony's assurances that it would be cooler here than in the city, the air hit them like a furnace when they opened the front door. The hermit's cottage was sheltered by a few old pines, and an ancient window air conditioner helped keep the interior temperature down, but outside was a yellow glare of dust and sun. Jordan's scowl deepened.

"Come on," Tony urged. "We'll get up behind the cottage where you can see the water."

Jordan followed, dragging his feet and muttering something under his breath, and Tony just led the way because he didn't know what else to do. The kid was scaring him, and he felt like he needed to do something but didn't have a clue what. Not leave him in front of the TV thinking, anyway. He was pretty sure Richard would have agreed with this plan.

Pretty sure.

A dirt track wound up the bluff behind the cottage and then over a rise, taking them to the sheer drop of the cliffs and the bay far below. Jordan stopped and stared, impressed despite himself. A warm breeze blew in their faces, but Tony had been right: the wind coming off the water was cooler.

"Not bad, huh?" Tony asked.

Jordan grunted in response. Below, they could see some of the house kids exploring tracks down the cliff side. It was a wild prospect, wilder than in the fishing village—Tony could see caves dotting the cliffs to the north and the tangled, rocky path of a landslide to the south. Laughter and chatter from the explorers floated up from below. He didn't know what Dr. Smith and Susan Brown had told them about their sudden relocation, but whatever it was, most of the kids were doing a good job of embracing the adventure.

He looked at Jordan and saw, alarmed, that the boy's face had gone blank again. Was he hearing something? Seeing something?

Nothing good, if he was.

Tony smacked him in the arm, a friendly gesture but meant to jar him out of whatever head space he was in, and pointed to a steep trail winding down. "Let's go," he said. "Looks like fun."

"You're not supposed to take me out from under the shield," Jordan said.

Why did that sound like a challenge?

"I'm not," Tony said, growing irritated. "The shield extends down there. Now come on. You need to get some exercise."

Jordan looked like he was about to retort, but he didn't. Instead, he picked his way forward, and with a scowl over his shoulder at Tony, started down the steep path.

Tony followed, pleased. About time the kid just went for it. He still wasn't sure what he hoped to accomplish out here, other than distracting the boy.

The path wasn't easy to follow. It was steep, and interrupted with roots and nettles and the low, sweeping branches of tangled pines growing out of the cliff side. The air grew cooler as they descended, but the exertion of keeping their feet drew a sweat from them both, and neither spoke. Tony got the distinct impression that Jordan was mad at him anyway, or at least highly irritated, and tried not to feel completely irritated back. He was supposed to be the older, more mature one, right? So he should have some patience?

Something like that, yeah.

The bay stretching out before them was blazingly blue, glaring up at them under the sun. A haze farther out on the water softened it, and Tony thought over all the plans they'd discussed in the fishing village and wondered whether Chris was out on the water with Mary and April and David.

He swallowed a lump in his throat.

They had never been close, but David had been the closest thing to a father he'd had for most of his life. It wasn't easy, the betrayal. He kept his mind mostly focused on chasing demons and fighting and helping Reese, and didn't think too much about the personal impact of David's turning his back on all of them. Actually hating them. Trying to kill them.

It sucked.

Jordan had stopped. Tony almost walked right into him, pulled forward by the sharp downward slope. "What?" he asked.

Jordan pointed to the left, south. Another path followed a level ridge, twisting a bit, and looked like it eventually led to a cave.

"Yeah, that's cool," Tony said. "You want to explore?"

Jordan just rolled his eyes and headed up the path, leaving Tony to follow, grumbling to himself. The kid's bad attitude was rubbing off.

The air outside the cave was foul, like something had died inside. Jordan looked like he was going to go inside anyway, but just before he ducked through the opening, a raven overhead cawed.

They both stopped and looked up. The bird was huge, sitting on a gnarled branch of pine about four feet up. It stared right at them for a moment and then spread its black wings and lifted off, hovering on an ocean breeze before flapping away.

Jordan seemed frozen in his tracks.

Tony watched the bird fly away, wondering why he felt so unnerved by the encounter.

Jordan turned on his heel and started back the way they had come, pushing past Tony.

"Hey!" Tony called. "Don't you want to explore the cave?" He knew it stank, but still ... he wouldn't have let that stop him as a boy.

"No."

"Why not?"

"I just don't okay?" Jordan was climbing back up the path toward the cottage, moving faster than he had on the downslope. Tony hurried after him. What was ...

He stopped.

The bird.

He hadn't thought to look closely, to see if it could have been possessed.

That wasn't uncommon. The demons wanted bodies, needed them for a lot of things. Animals were less useful than humans, but still animate, and easier to possess. Birds, with their good eyesight and ability to get close to humans without alarming anyone, were especially common hosts.

And the way Jordan was high-tailing it back to the cottage ...

"Hey!" Tony called, unhappy with how much distance the boy was putting between them. "Wait up!"

Jordan didn't. If anything, he sped up even more. But Tony increased his own speed and closed the gap between them, his lungs burning from the fast jog straight uphill.

"Was that a demon?"

No answer. Jordan was still climbing.

"Kid, come on! I need to know. Was that a demon?"

Jordan swivelled his head and looked at him, his eyes wide and his face pale. Still no answer. He looked away and kept going.

But Tony had seen what he needed to know. He clambered up after Jordan, keeping the space between them tight, so he could hear the boy's laboured breathing and see how spooked he still looked.

"Did it talk to you?" Tony asked.

Still no answer.

Tony stopped and put out his hand, grabbing Jordan's shoulder and pulling him to a halt. "I need to know," he said.

"I'm trying to take care of you. All of you."

"You shouldn't have brought me down here," Jordan said, and he pulled away and kept going.

When they got to the cottage, they were greeted by bad static and tinny laughter. This time Alicia was watching TV, and Angelica was hanging out in the stamp-sized kitchen next to it, looking through cupboards full of glass bottles stopped with corks. A few sported nearly unintelligible labels. Most weren't labeled at all. She threw Tony a look when he entered, pointing to the bottles. "How old was that hermit? I think maybe I found the elixir of life."

"Angelica, something's up," Tony said, closing the cupboard in front of her. She protested, but he ignored her. Jordan had gone straight to the TV, sitting next to his sister and hugging his knees to his chest.

"We saw a demon," Tony said. "Jordan and me. In a bird."

"Why were you out?" Angelica asked. "You were supposed to keep him here."

"I know. Look, I just took him down the cliff a little ways. He was sitting here thinking too much and it wasn't good for him."

"Richard told you to keep him in the house."

"Richard isn't here," Tony said, frustrated and annoyed that she was fixating on his actions instead of listening to his news. "He would have understood why I took him out. But there was a demon down there. I thought the shield was supposed to keep them out."

"Not necessarily out. Just powerless."

"How powerless?" Tony asked.

"I don't know. Relatively. April said the man who came into the village house was in his own right mind ... well, sort of. But the demon couldn't control him there. Or empower him."

"Well, something freaked Jordan out, and I don't think it was the sight of a bird. I think it talked to him."

She lowered her voice. "Is he okay?"

"No. Richard was right. He's being pulled back. I'm glad the bird scared him so much—maybe the scare will throw him back our way for a little while. But it's not going to last. He needs to join us, or he is going to go back to them."

Tears filled her eyes. "I hate that.'

"Me too. But it's true." He glanced around the cottage, but there was no sign of anyone except the children and Angelica. "Where is everyone else?"

"Miss Brown took them on a nature walk."

"And she left you two here?"

Angelica shrugged. "We're being punished, I think."

"What did she tell the other kids, anyway?"

"Some song and dance about going on a retreat."

He frowned. "I'd rather they knew the truth. I think it would be easier to keep them safe."

"Maybe." She wrinkled her brow. "You think we're going to have to keep them safe? I mean, besides just keeping them here under the shield?"

"I don't think that raven was just a freak appearance,"

Tony said.

"Could Jordan have called it here?"

"What do you mean?"

"I don't know, exactly. But if he wants them back ... if he's getting restless and wants to be possessed again ... do they know that? Can they feel it? Maybe he's creating a crack in the shield."

Tony considered the possibility and didn't like how plausible it felt. "I don't know what to do about him. He's scared of the demons, but he's playing with the idea of still being on their side. He won't talk to me. I don't think he even likes me."

"Just keep trying," Angelica said. "You can't do anything else."

"I wish we were out on a boat," Tony said, glancing glumly at the four walls of the cottage. "Like Chris and Mary. Not stuck here."

"Birds can get out on the water too."

"Yeah," Tony said. "I hope they've thought of that."

"They're prepared," Angelica said. Then added, "As much as anybody."

"I wish I felt like we were." Tony heaved a sigh and sat down at the table, a square barely big enough for two people that sat on rickety legs and was covered with dusty dishes, half-empty bottles of who-knew-what, and dog-eared paperback books. He picked up one of the books and riffled through it. "This book is so old it's crumbling in my hand."

Angelica shoved aside a few dishes and sat across from him. Her chair creaked loudly under her. It seemed amazing the whole place hadn't fallen apart long ago—like even though the hermit had lived here, he hadn't really used anything or bothered to keep it up. "Do you think we should call everyone up here?" she asked. "Is an attack going to happen?"

"I don't . . . " he tried to think the question through. "I don't think so. I just saw one raven. And I think it came for Jordan—because he was calling it somehow or because it was just coming to call him. I don't think they can get through the shield in a major way."

"Okay then," Angelica said. "So don't stress. We'll just keep keeping an eye on everyone, and especially on those two in there"—she pointed toward the living room, with its obnoxious racket from the TV, which they had turned up too loud—"and we'll trust that everybody else is getting their jobs done and this battle is going to end well."

"Do you really think that's going to happen?"

"What else would happen?"

"We could lose."

She regarded him seriously. "It's true."

"But not likely."

She smiled. "Since when does the Oneness really lose?"

"Since when does the Oneness betray itself?"

The smile faltered. "Nothing has really changed. We're still out here watching out for each other and giving the demons hell. Nothing to worry about."

He grinned. "I like that. Just wish I didn't feel like I was sticking my fingers in my ears and singing la la la."

**Rachel Starr Thomson**

"My ears are open," Angelica said. "Yours too. Just because we've seen and heard some nasty things doesn't mean the whole world has changed. Have a little faith."

He nodded. She held up a bottle of something brown, corked and opaque behind thick glass. "And if you need a little extra help, you could try some of this stuff. Seems like it kept the hermit alive for a hundred years or something like that."

In the living room, someone on the TV shot someone else, and the sound, compounded by static, made Tony jump. Angelica laughed at him and shoved the bottle in his direction. "Yeah, you definitely need to take some of this."

**On the water,** the air was ten degrees cooler at least. The sun was blinding, glaring off waves the colour of white crystal.

The boys owned three boats: a skiff, a small fishing trawler with nets where they spent most of their time, and this one, a sailing yacht that was Chris's pride and joy.

He had never pictured using it as a floating prison cell, much less a floating interrogation unit. Or whatever exactly they had made it.

Never imagined giving his sleeping quarters—below deck— to a man who hated his guts and who hated everyone else he cared about.

Who had tried to turn his mother into some kind of monster.

Who had almost ruined the life of a girl he cared about, and tried to turn her too.

Begrudgingly, Chris had to admit that he wouldn't have

known Reese without David's crime against her. If she hadn't been exiled, she wouldn't have come to the village and thrown herself off the cliff, and he and Tyler wouldn't have found her, and discovering what she was wouldn't have led him to Mary and to finally, after all these years, hearing the truth about his father and his mother and the Oneness.

A truth he was resisting, and he didn't know why.

Tyler had gone over to the Oneness. It hadn't taken long at all. He'd recognized in them everything he longed for, everything he'd missed in life, everything Chris hadn't been able to give him no matter how much he wanted to or how much he tried. He'd accepted them in a moment, like it always seemed to happen, and become something that wasn't just human anymore.

His best friend, a . . . something.

Gulls called high overhead, circling under a few strips of stark white cloud. Chris watched them, his eyes tracing their circles, following the lines of their wings. He adjusted the sail to catch a brisk wind from the south and breathed in the air that braced him. This was where he belonged. His father had thrived out here. Diane had stayed near the water because of the memories and because she wanted Chris to follow in Douglas's footsteps, hoped that he would. Sailors and fishermen who had been Douglas's friends took Chris aboard when he was small, and he owned his first boat at twelve; when Tyler came along less than a year later, the boys spent every possible moment on the water. And grew up, finished high school, and decided that was where they wanted to stay—not moving on with the rest of the world, but salted and baptized by the ocean spray in the midst of their nets and their sails. They made a poor but livable income fishing and doing odd jobs around the docks—patching sails, mending hulls, packing catches in ice.

This was not the use he'd pictured for the yacht when he bought it for cheap and started work repairing it. But he was glad he could serve.

David was sitting in the stern, his arms folded, looking green beneath his six o'clock shadow and as miserable as ever. He glared at Chris when he noticed him watching. They had had a brief but lively discussion over whether to tie the man up—Chris and Diane for, April and Mary against—but ultimately had decided to leave him free. Chris felt like he'd chosen to let a viper loose in a garden where he'd be weeding all day, but he hoped that keeping an eye on the fugitive would be good enough. He wouldn't put it past the man to kill them all in cold blood, but he was stronger, even with his arm in a cast. At least, he hoped he was.

Disgruntled, he remembered Reese's story of being healed of her wounds by the hermit on Tempter's Mountain, and he wished the old man was still alive so that he could fix his arm.

Not very selfless, are you? Chris asked himself. Wishing a man back from the dead just so you don't have to wear a cast.

He realized he was glaring back at David, a glare meant to show off all his strength and promise a beating if he ever caught him up to anything.

He was acutely aware of the women on the ship, all of whom were below in the cabin right now, and of his task: protect them at all costs.

David had turned his glare away; he was staring up, up at the gulls and the wisps of white in the blue sky. Out here the sun didn't beat like it did on shore. Chris could feel it burning the skin of his face and nose, but without the relentless weight of heat that had accosted them on land.

April appeared at his elbow. She was surprisingly good at moving quietly and quickly, even on the water where her footing was unsteady. She asked a few questions, and Chris showed her how to set the sail. He liked April, he had decided. Which was a good thing—it was hard enough not to wish she was Reese. If he had disliked her, it would be unbearable.

He left April handling the sail and stalked over to David, who looked up at him with the same unveiled enmity he'd been showing since the prison.

"You like it out here?" Chris asked.

"You didn't come over here to make conversation. Threaten me, like you're leading up to."

Chris wanted to kick him. He refrained. David stretched out, folding his hands on his stomach and closing his eyes in a gesture that dismissed Chris completely. "Tell Mary to get up here and talk to me," David said. "That's why we're here. Let's get it out of the way so you can get on to what you really want to do, what you have to do."

He knew David was referring to killing him.

Unbelievable that he could talk about it that way.

He thought of a few clumsy retorts but didn't say any of them.

"I'm here," Mary said from behind him, making him jump. He mumbled something and stepped aside, letting her come alongside him.

She looked down at David and shook her head lightly. His eyes were still closed.

"Ignoring me now?" she asked.

"Giving you all the attention you deserve," he answered without moving.

She sighed.

This was going to be a long trip.

April was watching them closely from her station across the deck, and Chris found himself drawn back to her, away from the tension between Mary and David.

"So where are we going?" she asked when he reached her side.

"Absolutely nowhere," he told her. "We're going to keep going in circles until we're finished with him."

One way or another.

The gulls were calling louder overhead, and April raised her eyes toward them, watching them. She looked worried.

"What?" he asked.

"Do you think they're demons?"

He had thought of it. "Naw."

"Do you think they'll come?"

"They might. We're doing our best to cut David off from help, but we can't seal off the sky."

She glanced down at the waves. "Or the sea."

"Attack of the fish?"

She made a face at him. "You never know."

He held up an oar. "I'll be ready. Beat them off with my paddle."

She laughed, and he was glad; glad to be making someone smile. But her expression sobered again quickly as she looked up at the birds again. "If they do come, I'll wish we had Reese with us. Or Richard. Mary is really the only fighter."

"You can fight, can't you? Wield that sword like all the rest of you? Even Tyler can do that."

"I can. But fighting isn't my gift—and I hate it."

He remembered that she had killed a man last time she bore the sword, and his heart went out to her.

"You know you did what you had to do."

"He didn't leave me any choice." She knew exactly what he was referring to. "I only wanted to drive the demon—or demons—out. He refused to let go. And he would have killed us. Not just me."

"I know."

"So many people have died."

And this time her eyes had strayed back to David, who was still reclining on the deck as though he had chartered this boat for a pleasure cruise. Mary sat near him, but far enough away to look like she was protecting herself. They weren't speaking.

"You know," Chris said, "everyone acted like we were getting the exciting job. I think the biggest risk out here might be that we get bored to death."

"Things will get exciting," April said. "Soon enough."

And she eyed the birds again.

"They aren't demons."

"You don't know that."

He looked up, watched them circling, heard their calls, and admitted that she was right.

He didn't know that.

\* \* \* \*

The best thing about driving a long way was that it gave one time to pray. The most frustrating thing about it was that even though you could pray, your attention had to be fractured, and you couldn't really enter in. Over the years Richard's gift for prayer had grown into an addiction; he craved the rush it gave him almost as much as the insight and power. It reminded him that he was transcendent, something more than just flesh and blood and bone, something more than anyone could see. At times like this, especially, with a battle hanging in the air and importance riding on everything he did and every word spoken, he needed that sense of transcendence.

He had been surprised when Alicia told him where they would go to meet with the woman, the one they were responsible to turn against the Oneness. It was a good three-hour drive, and he wondered who had chauffeured them on a regular basis.

Or if they'd found some other way to get around. Horrible as demonic possession was, it did offer attractive power to some, especially to those who would pursue it, like Clint had. And these children had been under his tutelage to some degree, and under David's direction. David, with his calculated plans, would have encouraged them to seek out the limits of power and use it.

It was very possible they'd travelled in the same way Alex had when he disappeared from Dr. Smith's house. He didn't like to think about the children being that well-versed in the practices of the demonic, but that was the whole point—they had been recruited, at their age, because their age and the ideal of innocence would make it so hard for the Oneness to fight them. Even to wrap their heads around fighting them.

Richard shook his. He was thinking of the children as enemies. They weren't, not anymore. Not for now. Thank God.

Please God they could keep it that way.

He comforted himself by remembering the presence of the cloud up on Tempter's Mountain. He hadn't really left the children in the care of two teenagers who were good at wielding a sword but mostly unproven at anything else.

The drive took him south, and he drove over a ridge to look down on a valley, split by a wide river spanned by highway and railroad bridges in three places, crowned by the high skyline of Mark. It was the biggest city in the region, dwarfing Lincoln, a one-time mining town that had grown and eventually been taken over by banking and tech companies. The heat outside swelled as Richard took the freeway into the city, looping around the heart of it, exacerbated by concrete and glaring off skyscraper glass. Billboards studded the roadway, trying to grab his attention away from the heavy, too-fast traffic, advertising concerts, TV shows, and toothpaste.

One did grab his attention for a moment, showing him the face of the woman he was going to see.

He slowed a little to get a better look, sobered.

David knew what he was doing.

His exit put him into the heart of the downtown arts district, and he poked through heavy traffic before finding a parking garage and heading into the sweltering heat in search of the box office and a concert ticket.

He had no idea how he was going to get access to her. That, he was leaving up to the plan—to the leading of the Spirit that was beyond his comprehenion but which he knew would come, opening doors in the right time and place.

Two steps into the lobby of the theatre, crowded with people, and he could feel a sword forming invisibly in his hand. He didn't call it all the way to being, but took note of the pressure and what it meant.

He should have known he wouldn't be alone.

That he could count on opposition as much as he could count on the Spirit to lead.

The lobby was a narrow, curved foyer open to three floors, with balconies looking down on it and glass windows letting in the sun and the presence of the city outside. Air conditioning kept the air comfortable, remarkable considering the heat outside and the hundreds of people crammed into the building, waiting for the doors to open. Richard stood in a corner and scanned the crowd, looking for signs of the enemy or anything else worth seeing. He spotted neither. The demonic was present; he could feel that in the sword in his hand; but lying low. People milled under hanging banners advertising other concerts, ballets, and plays; their chatter and laughter filled the air.

The doors open with a rush of cold air, and the crowd surged forward. Richard found his seat, in the balcony and toward the back, and settled in between a talkative woman and an overweight, surly gentleman taking notes on a yellow pad. The woman, thankfully, ignored him after a greeting and directed her attention to the people she was with.

Richard waited, listening.

He had a sense that the atmosphere itself was trying to talk to him, to tell him something, but he couldn't quite make out the message.

The curtains swept aside, and the spotlight lit a grand piano and a woman.

She was young, tall, blonde hair swept up in an elegant French roll. She wore a long, black dress, but it impressed Richard with its unremarkable quality: she wasn't there to call attention to herself, but to the music.

And that, she did superbly.

The music quieted all the buzz and energy of the crowd and called it up to something higher, alternately swelling and quieting, weeping and laughing, charging and comforting. The compositions were a mix: some classical, some original. Richard found the originals called to him more deeply, perhaps because they came from the same place his heart was at home: from the Spirit, from the Oneness. But he was as drawn by the woman as by the music. She didn't seem separated from it, a creator sharing her creation. They were one, her and the music that poured out of her. It was her spirit speaking, pouring out, beautifying, challenging.

He wondered if anyone in this crowd really heard it.

He was very sure his neighbours on either side, the woman who was quivering with her desire to talk and the critic taking notes and liberally blotching his paper with ink from a runny pen, did not.

He knew something intuitively as he listened, though, and that was that something was missing. That her music was meant to accomplish something it wasn't, to extend an invitation she was withholding. It was meant to sing, he understood, of the Oneness, and it was not.

She was holding that back deliberately.

Before the concert ended, he got up and excused himself, annoying other members of the audience as he slipped past them in the darkness. He murmured apologies and made his way toward an exit.

He walked outside, back into the heat and the noise of the city, feeling like had left a sacred place and descended into Hades. He still wasn't sure what he was going to do.

Following some instinct, or just wandering because he didn't know what else to do, he followed the contours of the building, down a dark alley, and came out by the stage exit. A black car was sitting there, waiting.

The driver was possessed.

He saw it immediately, like a flare in the air over the driver's half of the car. The sword appeared in his hand, fully formed, sharp and ready.

He did not think the man was equally aware of him.

He approached the car cautiously, but not too slowly; he didn't want to give the man extra time to notice him. The air buzzed as he drew closer. Hive. This was one of David's men. He was sure of it.

He knocked on the window, and the man rolled it down with a look of surprise—quickly replaced by recognition.

Richard drove the sword through the man's chest before he could act.

The demon wailed but released quickly, and the man slumped down behind the wheel. Richard reached through the open window to pop the lock on the door and dragged the man's body out, depositing him safely behind a dumpster to recover and absconding with his chauffer's coat and hat. Both made the sweltering heat worse, but he slipped into the car feeling grateful. His heart was racing with adrenaline.

He hoped she would come out before the chauffeur recovered.

His sword was still in his hand, and he laid it across his lap and kept a sharp eye on the rearview and side mirrors. The demon, bereft of a body, did not reappear.

He didn't know how long he would have to wait.

Calming himself as much as he could, taking one deep breath after another, he kept his eyes open and alert and tried to pray. To create a shield, an atmosphere. Something he could welcome her into so they could talk. Doing so was a challenge he wasn't sure he was up for; he was too on edge. The lobby had been full of demons—not hive demons, but enemies nonetheless. The whole city was likely full of them, as most cities were. And he was trying to whisk away their prime target.

For a moment, he allowed himself to close his eyes and center on the Spirit.

Whatever else, he knew he could not do this alone.

**Despite having lived by the sea** for nearly twenty years, Mary had never really spent time on it. It took her a few hours to get comfortable with the rhythm of the waves and the smell and weight of the salt spray, much heavier out here than in the village. David didn't seem to have the same luck; he stayed green well after her stomach had adjusted. His strategy for dealing with his situation seemed to be to wait, hands folded and eyes closed, like a man expecting an execution or taking a nap.

It made Mary angrier than she could explain to herself.

He was so normal to look at—so middle-aged and average—that she had to keep telling herself how evil he was, and recalling all the scenes that had played out before her eyes since he was discovered: his exile of Reese, his shooting the hermit on Tempter's Mountain, his dragging them all off to be killed at the warehouse, and his later presence in the house alongside Clint where Tyler and Chris were nearly murdered. She had to remind herself that he had something to do with children and teenagers being possessed, and that he had found the most evil people he could, and the most threatening demonic entities he could get power over, and pulled them together into a hive with the aim of infiltrating and destroying the Oneness.

All that, and she could swear he was snoring.

Humanity, she thought, you are strange.

So much power and passion in skin and bones, with a stomach to go queasy on the water and sinuses to snore under the influence of sleep.

She tried, too, to pull to mind the events of twenty years ago, the events David said had turned him, events he said she had been involved in. You brought me into the Oneness, he had told her. You were there when I turned against it.

But she didn't know what he was talking about.

The metal rings on the sail tapped against the mast with a tink, tink, tink, and she looked up at it and the blue sky beyond, wracking her memory.

Was she crazy somehow?

Had she blocked it from her memory?

There were plenty of horrible memories from those days. Plenty that could have turned a man. Plenty that could have made his heart go cold and even full of hate. But that wasn't how she remembered any of it. In all the destruction, and betrayal and cruelty, and demonic enterprise and death, she remembered the Oneness drawing closer together. She remembered unity strengthened and fired by affliction, new members—like Diane and nearly Douglas—coming in, death being shown up for the sham it ultimately was when you were One. That was what she remembered of those days: that she had never seen the Oneness so clearly, or known her own place in it so proudly, or believed in it so passionately.

David's experience had been different, evidently.

And she had been there.

There were birds in the sky again, flying near the boat, soaring and diving to fish. April and Chris, at the far end of the yacht, were eyeing them nervously. She knew they feared a demonic attack—and it might come that way, from the air. But she feared far more that it would not. She feared that she would be uninterrupted in her talk with David—whenever it really began—and they would say all there was to say, and he would not repent.

And they would have to kill him.

Because they could not allow the hive to go on.

They could not allow him to continue to threaten the Oneness the way he had, and did.

But . . .

She closed her eyes. Shook her head at the thought. Felt the cold chill of it fall over her.

To kill one of their own.

To deliberately take his life, even in justice, even in fair retribution for the lives he had taken and the lives he had ruined.

What would it mean to them?

Would it cripple them—change their unity somehow?

Could the Oneness even survive it?

She cleared her throat to open conversation, but he didn't acknowledge her or move.

Maybe he really was sleeping.

The sail cast shade across his face and the pile of netting he was lying on. She struggled to remember that face younger.

All her clear memories of David were from more recent years. She knew him as head of the Lincoln cell. The fishing village was quiet; they rarely crossed paths. When they did, there was the quiet sympathy of leadership; they both knew what it was to watch out for others and try to steer them, even more than was the usual lifestyle of Oneness. She had considered him a friend.

But before that . . .

What was before that?

She was still trying to struggle through that when Chris strode up and, without warning, kicked David in the side. The man rolled over and glared up without a yell. He'd been awake, then.

"Chris!" Mary burst out.

He looked down at her, his eyes smoldering, but didn't answer. Then he turned his gaze back to David. "Time to wake up," he said. "Mary's here to talk to you. And I'm not out here just to give you a nice long nap."

"We don't have much to talk about," David said, looking at Mary.

"Talk about the Oneness. Talk about what you're trying to do to it."

"You care a lot for someone who refuses to join," David said. "Watch your interest in that girl, Christopher. Oneness women will lead you places you don't want to go."

Chris flushed. "Shut up."

"You told me to talk."

"To Mary." He seemed to realize he was being drawn into a childish word game, and he glared at David again. Then to Mary, "I didn't kick him hard. Wish I had."

"Chris, you had better go steer the ship," she said, noting the weariness in her own voice.

Weary already, and this hadn't even really begun.

Chris turned away with a last glare at David and stalked back across the ship. For all that she knew he didn't need to steer anything—they were really just drifting out here, and didn't plan to do anything else for a while—she was grateful for his obedience and more grateful for his presence.

So amazingly much like having Douglas with them.

Diane was below. She had not come up yet, burying her nose in a paperback—a novel, of all things, at a time like this—and saying little to Mary or anyone else.

It wasn't really fair that she should have to be part of this fight, but she was Oneness—and Oneness could not isolate.

Not even if they wanted to.

"Chris is right," Mary said. "We didn't bring you out here for a nap."

"You brought me out here to kill me," David said gamely. "So why don't you do that?"

"We don't want to kill you, David."

"You should. You should want to eradicate the evil that is me. Do I have to remind you what I've done? And that's not even all. I could tell you a lot more."

She wondered if she should pursue that line of conversation. He might tell her something that would help Richard or the others.

But somehow she doubted it. David was all about control. He was not going to give that up just for the sake of goading her.

"That's not really what I care about," Mary said.

"Oh, that's right. Because you care about me, yes? Like the Oneness cares about every individual. So much that you invite us all to be lost in the conglomerate and suffer all our lives under the impossible burden of unity when we were made to strive, to be ourselves, fully ourselves, to make ourselves. To realize what we are supposed to be, like I can never do, because I have you and all the rest tied to my ankle like a millstone."

"Oneness is what we're supposed to be," Mary said. "You know that." She regretted those words instantly. "Or maybe you don't. I don't know what you know anymore—what lies you've let twist your mind. So maybe you don't know anything. But Oneness is not a loss, David. It's a coming into yourself—into who you are meant to be."

She brightened just a little at the idea that maybe, just maybe, he only needed to hear this again. That maybe he just needed to be reminded of the truth.

"If you would just embrace that," she said. "If you would just stop striving against it, you'd see. Oneness would allow you to be all you are. It would allow you to embrace your life and your destiny. You never can if you try to do it on your own."

"But I'll never know that, one way or the other, because Oneness refuses to let me go."

She looked away, over the water. She couldn't handle looking into his face right now—the pallor, the anger, the bitter, bitter cold. The wind was brisk and raising white caps in the distance, but here the water was relatively calm. She marveled at tides and currents, at the way it could all be one ocean and yet affected so differently in different places just yards away. And she tried to put herself in David's place, just for a moment.

"What is it like?" she asked.

This time—maybe for the first time—she caught him off-guard.

"Excuse me?"

"What is it like—being held by the Oneness when you don't want to be? What do you experience that as? I know what Oneness is to me. I don't know what it is to you. I can't fathom it—can't imagine it." She turned her eyes back to him and looked him in the eye after all, gratified that she had raised something in them that wasn't the controlled, calculated freeze and taunt of a few minutes ago.

"It's a never-ending fire," he said. He sat up, suddenly, loosing his hands and leaning forward, close to her, his face close to her face. "It burns every minute. It's noise that never ceases, when all I want is to be alone. It's guilt that never dies away. Every time I try to dream, every time I want to hope, Oneness is a million voices and a million threads pulling me away from myself, scattering me, forcing me to care when I do not want to. It is the weight of the world—of the universe—when all I want is to be light and to be free."

She considered his words.

She did not want to, but this was the first time she'd felt like she was seeing the man behind the monster of betrayal. She owed it to him to consider his words.

"Come now," he said, very softly. "You can go deeper than that."

Her eyes fluttered open—she hadn't realized she'd shut them. "What?"

"You're thinking about what I said. But you're holding yourself back. We are still One, you and I. You can go deeper. You can feel what I feel, if you'll just care enough to enter in. I haven't invited anyone into my spirit in two decades, Mary. I'll invite you. You really want to know the key to all this? Come in."

She closed her mouth—she was gaping.

"No," she rasped.

He sat back, smug—but perhaps disappointed, too.

Perhaps even hurt.

"You're afraid to," he said. "We are all One. We are all meant to share in one another's souls, one being, one body in heaven and earth. But you are too afraid to enter into what it is to be me."

He closed his eyes and folded his hands again, the posture of sleep. "My soul is too dark. So I am One, and I am completely alone."

Never alone.

The words were the watchword of the Oneness, the words the Spirit whispered when you first joined, the words that were promise and strength and new being.

Never alone.

But he was.

And her heart moved with compassion.

He did not open his eyes. "I feel that, you know. You all think I'm cold and hardened, but I feel Oneness acutely. I know you are pitying me. And I also know how afraid you are."

She stood, almost thrown off balance by the waves, and grabbed the rigging to steady herself. Her breath was coming fast. She turned on her heel and almost threw herself down the short, narrow stairway into the cabin. She leaned against the wall and tried to slow her breathing down.

From the bed, Diane looked up over the ratted pages of a mystery novel, the cover looking damaged by damp. She raised her eyebrows and then lowered her glance back to the pages before speaking.

"He's getting to you?"

"He's . . . I don't know."

"He's dangerous. He's getting to you."

Mary didn't answer.

"You shouldn't have brought me," Diane said. "I can't help you with this. I look at him and just want to kill him for what he's done, and then I sympathize with him. I wouldn't mind out of the Oneness myself, sometimes."

"You have a role," Mary said faintly. "You'll find it."

"You, on the other hand, are going about this badly. You're not going to win this playing war as usual."

"I'm not sure what you mean."

Diane sighed and put the book down on the bed beside her. "What's getting to you?"

"That I can't remember . . . that he's goading me with something I seem to have forgotten all about. That he can read me like a book."

"That he's playing with you," Diane said.

"Yes." She almost laughed, hopeless. "He told me to come in . . . to form a deeper connection with him and go plunging into his heart. I can't."

Diane fingered the book like she wanted to disappear back into it, but didn't. She fixed Mary with a steady gaze, a challenge in it.

"Tyler walked," she said.

"What?"

"Tyler walked. Tyler used the power of the Oneness and walked when he should have been paralyzed by the drugs he was on, and Tyler is new to the Oneness and not that good at anything. But he reached out and did a miracle and saved a lot of lives."

"Yes, he did," Mary said, lost.

"And yet you're afraid to use your power. You can form a deeper connection with David."

"Yes . . ."

"Then why don't you do it?"

She shuddered.

"You're afraid of what you'll find there," Diane said. "But you're a soldier, aren't you? You can't just stay out of enemy territory because it might be dangerous. It is dangerous. This is war." She frowned. "When you talked me into the Oneness all those years ago, you did it by painting a picture of a world that was supernatural, where we could all become more than ourselves, where anything could happen. But you don't live like that world really exists. Yes, you're good to others—good to me, good to your cell. Unusually good. But you're ignoring a whole lot of power."

Mary blinked and lowered her eyes to the smoothly polished floor.

Was she right?

David frightened her more than anything on earth. She would have faced a battalion of demons before she would go exploring his heart. And yet he was her brother. He was Oneness. He knew her like she refused to know him. And maybe he frightened her so much not just because of what he was, but because of what she was.

Because he was challenging her to find out what she was.

Maybe, just maybe, she had buried herself in the Oneness after all. How had he put it? Lost in the conglomerate.

Not because it had to be that way, not because the Oneness demanded it, but because she wanted it—wanted the safety of numbers and anonymity and being one more component in a great machine.

A body, she reminded herself.

But what good was a body part that didn't function properly? Or to its highest potential?

She looked up and fixed her eyes on the deck.

"You're going to do it, aren't you?" Diane asked. She hadn't moved—or picked her book back up.

Mary just looked at her, and after a moment nodded slowly.

She ascended the stairs feeling like she was walking off a precipice. Spray met her as she came out into the air again, wetting her hair and clothes. The water was cold, but in the hot air that hardly registered; it felt alive and made her feel alive.

She wondered what she would leave behind by entering into David's world with him.

His expression changed as she approached this time—somewhere between elation, surprise, and fear.

"You're going to do it, aren't you? You're going to come in?"

"I need to know what you know," Mary said. "And feel what you feel."

"So you can rescue me? So you can pull me back out?"

"Yes."

"You know that, once you've been in my soul, it might be you who need rescuing."

"I know."

"No one else will come in after you. I've been with Oneness for twenty years, and no one has ever dared go that deep. You have power, you know—we all do. And no one uses it."

"Not no one."

"Who does? Richard? He buries himself away in prayer. Speaks with power but never pushes the limits, never seeks to be all he is. The hermit I killed? He was even worse—cut himself off from the rest of you, for all intents and purposes. Because he was too strong, and too afraid of his strength. Some other nameless, faceless millions, all over the globe? They're all like you. Every single one I've seen is like you—using your power to stay low and lose yourself in the mass instead of distinguishing yourselves in any way. The Oneness are fools. They pretend to embrace great power and terrible reality and then spend their whole lives hiding from both."

She almost smiled. "You sound like an apologist. Like one arguing for the Oneness, not against it."

"I would, if I didn't hate it so much. I don't want to be great on your terms. I want to be great, or at least to exist, on my own. And you—you all—have denied me that forever. That doesn't mean I can't see what you do not: that the Oneness truly is power."

He leaned back, but his eyes didn't take on their early languidness. They were sharp, bright. He was interested now. "The demonic are different. They exult in, bathe in, play in power. It is everything to them. Imagine if you were to do the same, how much would be available to you."

"Power is not our goal, or our lifeblood," Mary said. "Love is."

"Well then," David said, smirking, "come inside and love me where it's real. You know you can. You know you must. Do it."

* * * *

**Attack** 131

The woman got into the car escorted by bodyguards, but they did not stay with her, instead fanning out to the rest of the alley and ensuring the car got out without a hitch. Richard pulled his cap low over his eyes and pulled the car out smoothly, raising his hand in a friendly signal to the bodyguards that all was well—dearly hoping it would work.

The moment she entered the car, he felt all that her music had aroused in him. He knew her, knew her heart and soul, knew how passionately she believed in higher things and how deeply she wanted to call others. He also felt the conflict: whatever it was that held her back. Stopped her from issuing invitation to the Oneness, stopped her short of being what she was.

He eased the car into traffic without saying a word, just checking in the rearview to ensure his passenger was real, was really there, and was all right. She was more beautiful up close than she had been on stage, simple and elegant. She seemed distracted, staring out the window in a way that betrayed agitation.

He didn't think she would notice if he went the wrong way.

Not that he didn't want to take her home—he just didn't know where that was supposed to be.

Guessing, he headed back to the freeway. He had some idea where the wealthier apartments and condos were; hopefully she was staying somewhere in that district.

To his surprise, she noticed.

"You're going the wrong way," she said abruptly. He didn't respond.

She leaned forward and tapped him on the shoulder. "Kevin. You're going the wrong way. We're in the penthouse this time, remember?"

He cleared his throat, debating whether to actually turn his face for a moment, but in the time it took him to ask that question, she got over her distraction and really saw the man in front of her.

"You're not Kevin," she blurted, with surprising calm, and two seconds later, "You're Oneness."

"True, and true," Richard said. "My name's Richard. My apologies for the unconventional introduction, but I need to talk to you."

He was impressed that she didn't seem startled or intimidated. There was in her an openness he hadn't expected from someone David was targeting. The others he had gone after—Diane, Jacob, even Reese—had been hardened to some degree, had thrown up walls. But openess seemed the primary characteristic of this woman's soul.

"The car isn't a good place to talk," she said. "I can steer you toward home if you're willing."

"I'll take you anywhere you want to go," he said.

"Good then. Get off that exit and turn around."

He obeyed. A quick glance in the rearview showed eyes that were alive with interest and curiosity. Far from being suspicious or cagey, she was treating him like a welcomed friend.

"Just a few exits up," she told him once they were back on the freeway going the other way, and then added, "What did you do with Kevin?"

"Gave him something of a hangover," Richard said, wondering how much to tell her. But then he decided to be as open with her as she was with him. "I set him free."

**Attack**          133

She was quiet at that, sitting farther back in the seat and pondering.

"How much do you know about me?" she asked.

"Very little. I know your name—Melissa. I know you're one of us." He lowered his voice. "And I know they're targeting you."

"Pull off here," she said softly, and directed him down a busy three-lane one-way street to a high-rise on the left, where he pulled into a parking garage, parked in the reserved spot where she told him to, and got out to open the door for her.

"Thank you," she said. She wavered a little on her high heels when she got out, and he put out a hand to steady her. She let him.

"You're very trusting," he said with a smile. "Most women don't like to be alone with strange men in a parking garage."

"You're not a strange man," she said. "You're one of us. Most men, I do not trust. You, I do."

He liked her. He liked her immensely. He wasn't sure he had expected that. He'd been counting on finding another Jacob or David—someone swallowed by her own twisted perspective or eaten up by hatred.

He wasn't expecting to find Melissa.

She led the way to the elevator and from there to the penthouse suite, but in such a way that he felt like he was leading, or at least doing more than following like a flunky. She passed her elegance on, endowing others with it, rather than making them feel low. He knew it was this way with everyone, not just him; he could feel that.

The penthouse was like her: elegant, simple. An open-concept apartment with windows on all four sides looking out over the city, it was uncluttered, graced with a few carefully selected paintings on the wall and furniture the colours of cream and wicker. She poured him a drink without asking and then seated herself on a love seat, gesturing for him to sit down across from her.

He did.

"What do you know about me?" she asked.

A slightly different question from the "how much."

His answer was much the same. "Very little. You are brilliant; I attended your concert this afternoon."

"Oh," she said, perking up and seeming pleased by that.

"And as I told you before—I know your name, that you are Oneness, and that they are targeting you."

"Who is this 'they'?" she queried, but he was fairly sure she knew the answer.

"The hive," he said grimly. "They've been sending you children. They're trying to turn you against us. I'm just not sure why or how."

For the first time, a troubled expression crossed her face. "I love the Oneness," she said. "I always have. I have been One since I was a child—six years old. My parents were One."

"Married? That's unusual."

"It was a blessing." She put her wine glass down and paused, as though pondering whether to tell him more. "The Oneness has been my whole life. When I began to play and to write music, it was with the express purpose of putting the Spirit's invitation into notes, where others could hear it audibly."

"But that's not what you played this afternoon," Richard said gently. "Forgive me, but while you expressed our ideals and our hope, you did not express the invitation. You backed off."

"I can't play it anymore."

"Why not?"

She lifted troubled blue eyes to him. "Because I'm not sure I believe in it anymore."

"You love the Oneness, it's your whole life, but you don't believe in it?"

"I am not sure I believe it is what it says it is."

He sighed. "Then I know why the hive is targeting you."

She stood and faced a window, looking out, folding her arms in front of her. "I don't like that word. Targeting. Like I have nothing to do with it. Maybe I am exploring."

He considered joining her but decided to give her space instead. She swept one arm out, encompassing the city. "Down there, what I see is two things: order and chaos. The Oneness and the darkness, the demonic. No?"

"It's an apt picture."

She turned. "Then tell me why the Oneness cannot give me order, and the demonic can."

"I'm not sure I know what you mean by that."

"You mentioned the children. Do you know what they do when they come here?"

He didn't. "I have no idea what their visits to you look like."

She walked back to stand before him. "Then you probably also have no idea that I am dying."

Her words startled him so much that he physically jumped.

She sat down. "Cancer. I am told it's incurable. I am told I will die within a year."

"You don't look sick." It was a stupid thing to say, and he kicked himself.

"Nonetheless, my body, which is Oneness, which is supposed to be tapped into the Life beyond life and given strength and vitality by the tapestry of beings all across the world, is corrupt and corrupting. And I sought the Oneness for answers, I have prayed, I have tried to connect to the strength of others, and I have found no help at all."

Despite the force of her words, she did not look away or betray any undue discomfort. They might have been discussing music or a public event.

"But then the children started coming. Yes, I know they are possessed. But they are forcing me to rethink my beliefs about that. Because when they come, they are innocent—they are children. The demons only give them power."

Richard thought of the same children holding his hands at the house where Clint and David had tried to burn several of his friends alive, and he shuddered deep within. The face they had shown Melissa was only a partial one. There was always another side to the coin.

"They can heal," she continued. "When they come, I surrender to their power, and they heal me, bit by bit. The doctors confirm it. They don't know why I 'don't look sick,' as you told me. They don't know why the cancer isn't progressing like it should."

"But they have not told you that you're in remission?"

She hesitated. "Let me rephrase. The cancer is progressing. It's growing. But it's having no effect on me. The treatments I get from the children are canceling out its power. They are giving me life. Life the Oneness can't give."

"How often do they come?" he asked.

"Once a week."

"When are they due to come next?"

"In two days." She gave him a pointed look. "You're very much bothered by this."

"I am, yes." There was little point in hiding that. "You say you love the Oneness, yet you're betraying it."

"Perhaps not," she said. "If the Oneness is that which gives life, and it is not giving life, then perhaps the Oneness is corrupt and needs to be called back to purity. If what we call chaos is imparting wholeness, then perhaps we need to question our terms."

"Or," Richard said, "perhaps you are deceived, and your terms are skewed because your perspective is skewed."

"Life and death are rather clear. If one thing is giving me life, and another giving me death, it's not hard to see where the true power and goodness lies."

"That would be true," he said, slowly, aware that he was treading in deep waters, "if death was the end. But Oneness has always been the transcendence of death—the lasting beyond it. So death is not the ultimate evil."

For the first time, her face clouded, and he saw hurt and

defensiveness there. "That's easy for you to say when you are not facing it," she said.

"I have faced it. Recently. In battle with the demons."

"Good, then. Die in a glorious fight, convinced that you're a hero and your death is a blaze, and leave me to waste away and lose everything. My music—my purpose—everything. Not in a fight, just in corruption. I'm only thirty-three years old, Richard. I should not have to die like this."

He closed his eyes, unable to continue meeting the expression in hers, but he could not shut out their connection—the Oneness, the communion of souls that even now racked his with her pain and abysmal sense of loss, of waste.

He couldn't blame her for her questions. Couldn't even blame her for turning to the powers she had, when they offered her another way—a way to save herself, her work, and her sense of destiny.

David had been right to target her. She was enormously vulnerable because she was enormously gifted, because she cared more deeply than most people, Oneness or not, ever would.

He couldn't possibly tell her that he had taken her "healers" away. They would not be coming in two days. Maybe not ever again.

He saw that from her perspective, and winced. The Oneness had not only been unable to heal her. It had denied her the one source of healing she had found—had actively cut it off.

He couldn't say that.

He did say, and he wasn't even sure why he did, "I don't want you to die."

"Thank you," she said. "Likewise."

She smiled. "I believe you really do care. You're very sincere—I sensed that from the moment in the car when I realized what you were. And you have power of your own. You're a man of the Spirit like few are. I'm sorry that my questions, and my journey, are an affront to you."

He wanted to protest that, but in a sense she was right. She was questioning, actively pushing back, against everything he stood for.

"Did you know your driver was possessed?" he asked.

"Kevin? Of course."

"So the children aren't the only hive members you've had around."

She smiled, almost indulgently. "I've been questioning the reality of things. About what exactly the demonic is. So while I am unsettled about the answers, I'm practicing tolerance."

She leaned back and interlocked her long, slim fingers over her knee. "So, I'm afraid if you came to rescue me, it's not going to work. I have chosen what I'm doing. I'm not really open to being rescued."

He shook his head, smiling, and reached for the drink she had poured him. He needed it. "There are more than one of you, you know. It's an all-out attack, a strategy. David—"

He stopped. She looked puzzled.

"You don't know this side of the story, do you?"

She smiled. "You may as well tell me."

He nodded. "It's long. Or it feels long. But there's a man—

one of us. His name is David. Unlike you, he hates the One-ness. Something happened to him twenty years ago, we don't know what, that made him want to be free of us. He can't be, and he's become twisted—angry and bitter. He's the one who began the hive."

"I'm listening."

"Somewhere along the way, he decided that if the Oneness will not let him go, then he is going to destroy it. And he sees clearly what everyone else does not—that if the demonic and the Oneness come together, chaos will override. The Oneness will became an agent of darkness, not only not holding the world together or combating darkness as it should, but actively spreading it. Death will ultimately triumph."

She made a sound but didn't say anything. He kept going. "So he has done two things. First, he has gathered demons together under his leadership and organization, creating a hive—a conglomerate of humans and demons working together toward a single goal. The children are part of that hive. So are . . . others. Others who are much more obviously evil. He's been careful. This hive has many faces."

She took a sip of wine and waited for him to continue. But he could see a wall up behind her eyes—she was not truly open to some of what he had to say.

"Second, he is going after members of the Oneness he sees as weak, trying to turn them. He wants to turn the Oneness against itself, infect it from within—transform it into a parody, a monster where once there was a man."

"You're poetic."

"I'm telling the truth. David himself is the first—and he's

worse than anything I've seen from the purely demonic. There's another man, called Jacob, very different but also frightening. He's been responsible for the deaths of several men recently, and has been controlling the lives of others—control, not unity, and not freedom. He's used fear and manipulation and isolation to create his own utopia. Not exactly Oneness ideals. I heard your music—I know you would never agree to the things Jacob does or believes."

"You are connecting me with him rather arbitrarily, don't you think?" she cut in.

"Not that arbitrarily. The children—" He stopped himself. He had almost told her what had happened, that he had driven the demons out and the children were no longer part of the hive—that he was keeping them in a secluded place, under a shield, where the demons couldn't even reach them.

Thereby destroying her victory over cancer.

"The children talked to me," he said slowly. "They told me that David has targeted you as well, and that they have been visiting you with the purpose of turning you against the Oneness. They aren't trying to lead you into truth or give you life. They're trying to use you. You told me you love the Oneness."

"I do."

"How much?"

Her face paled, and she looked away as her whole body went rigid.

They didn't speak.

But the question was clear.

How much?

Enough to suffer for that love?

Enough to die for it?

"You have no idea what you're asking me," she whispered.

She looked as though she would stand, perhaps to pace, but instead she trembled with profound weariness, and he saw not only the woman who had just played a concert for hundreds and moved them deeply, who had not only just spent herself in two hours of sheer artistry, who had not only opened her soul to a stranger and discussed things so deep they had to cost just to talk about, but who had been fighting a protracted battle for far too long.

She was tired. Weary.

He bowed his head. "I'm sorry. You're right. I think I should leave now. You need rest, and I . . . I can give you time to think about this."

"You don't have any choice about that," she said faintly.

He smiled. "It's true. But I'm glad to give you time. You said you love the Oneness, Melissa. I think I can say the Oneness also loves you."

He stood and reached out his hand. She looked at it a moment before taking it, and he helped her to her feet and steered her toward her room. He had no desire to leave her, but he knew he didn't have an option.

She turned just before she closed her bedroom door. "You'll stay nearby?" she asked.

"Yes," he said.

And he would.

**Jacob's directions took Reese** way off the highway and plunged them down a valley where it was noticeably cooler, shaded with old-growth trees that lined the roads and buzzing with bees and other insects. Beyond the trees, fields of wheat and corn waved in the sunlight. Giving up on the old air conditioner, she and Tyler rolled their windows down and let the fresh air flow in. Jacob didn't seem to notice. Impervious to the weather, he was a man on a mission.

That struck Reese as ironic. This was supposed to be their offensive, after all. They had pulled the man out of detention so they could somehow convert him, so they could accomplish their mission. Thus far they had been a giant failure, and he seemed more set in his ways than ever.

We have a week, she reminded herself. This is only day one. Rome wasn't built in a day.

Of course, it was highly possible he was thinking the same thing.

She had no idea where he was taking them. Maybe another commune like his. More proof that his way of doing life was worth any cost.

Instead, he told her to pull off the road outside a little iron gate. She did, the car lolling in the long weeds. He pushed through the gate, and she and Tyler followed, curious.

On the other side of a line of trees and tall weeds, they entered a manicured little cemetery.

Jacob strode to the centre of it, then turned and boomed, "What do you see?"

She had to admit he was better at this kind of thing than she was.

"A graveyard," Tyler said.

"Yes, a graveyard. And tell me what is memorialized here."

"Death," Tyler said, at the same time as Reese responded, "People's lives."

He eyes sparked. "I contend that the real answer is neither. What this place—and millions like it, all over the world—truly stands for is the failure of the Oneness."

Reese raised an eyebrow. "Big words for someone who has caused multiple deaths in the last couple of weeks."

"Now, now," he said, his tone dangerous, "I am innocent until proven guilty in this country. But guilty life is not the same as innocent life, and the death of the guilty is judgment, not failure—you understand the difference?"

"I understand that you see a difference."

"So you tell me," he said, booming again, ignoring her, "what does the Oneness stand for? What is it that we do?"

"Unity, love. We hold the world together."

"People say that. Do you mean it literally, or in some figurative sense?"

Reese considered that. "Both."

"You're right. Without the Oneness the world would in fact fly apart. Without the Oneness—the true Oneness—death and chaos would overtake everything, and the universe as we know it would cease to exist."

He turned to Tyler. "You see, boy? I am a believer. In every sense of the word, I believe in the Oneness, much more than many do. You did not join some weak straw man, some pretend game of men when you became One. You entered into the most serious business in the universe."

Tyler looked suspicious, but he listened. As did Reese.

"All right," Tyler said slowly. "We're here to stop death from reigning. But you think we should kill people. You don't make sense."

His eyes—those lively, dangerous eyes—glimmered. "What should die must die. That is how we will rid the world of chaos. Through judgment. When all judgment has been carried out, and everything corrupt is gone, there will only be life, and we will win. The fight will be over."

"You say that," Reese interrupted, "but you work with demons. They are evil, they are chaos, and you think you can somehow conquer darkness with their help?"

He shook his bearded head. "The demonic is power. That is all they are. They are agents of chaos and death only because we have not chosen to master them, to direct their energies elsewhere. We have used them as an excuse, that we should not have to be what we are. Because we are afraid to enter the fullness of our power, we are afraid of purity. We have compromised until we are sick, until we have become agents of corruption ourselves."

Reese shivered. "I still don't understand the graveyard."

He folded his arms and looked smug. "You will. Look around. Do you know anything about any of these people?"

With a wary look at him, Reese moved to read a gravestone. The name was not familiar; the date was within the last twenty years—more recent than she had expected in a place this out of the way.

As though he could read her mind, he said, "This is a private graveyard, fairly popular with wealthy people from Lincoln and Mark. It's not as old as it looks."

In testy obedience, she kept wandering, reading names, looking for one she knew. She found nothing.

When she stopped in front of an impressive granite headstone, carved with what looked like Greek pillars with serpents twined around them, Jacob said, "Stop."

She did. Tyler joined her, staring at the stone. "Creepy," he said.

Jacob came up behind them. "This is where my journey began," he said. "Twenty years ago. I knew this man."

The name on the stone was Franz Bertoller. Reese had never heard of him. According to the stone, he had been dead only four years.

"Twenty years ago?" she asked.

"He had selected his grave and had the stone carved in advance of his death. It was here before the final date was carved on it, ready to receive him. He died at a very old age—ninety-eight. Comfortable, happy, surrounded by family. 'Ancient and full of days,' as the old books put it."

He gave the speech with an edge, a foreboding tone that said he was about to reveal a dark mystery, and Reese found herself tense until he did.

"Few people ever knew it, but Franz Bertoller was responsible for one great act in his life. He did not push the buttons himself, but he arranged it all. He designed the hive. He bought the police."

Reese's stomach sank.

"He bombed a cell house and burned down two others, and then he hounded the Oneness in a massacre that those who were there have never forgotten. He unleashed hell. He advanced chaos. He was a murderer not of the wicked, but of the good. Our whole world sank deeper into darkness when his day of triumph came."

The serpents on the stone seemed more menacing now, more alive in the leafy shadows. Tyler and Reese were silent, staring at the stone.

"I had a wife," Jacob announced.

Startled, she turned and looked at him.

He continued. "Yes, I was one of the few Oneness who married, in the depth of unity and love that only those who are both One and in love can know. She was goodness, sweetness, purity itself—she was light. I loved her as no man has ever loved a woman."

His voice wavered as he spoke, and Reese believed him. He looked at them both with a passion and care that wrenched at her heart. "You may think I was hard on your friend—Chris. But I saw something. I saw that he was in love with one of ours, one of the Oneness, and that he was not yet One. I believe in love, Reese. I do not want you led astray by something that will only hurt you in the end. He needs to come into the Oneness. You know that. I was only trying to help him get there."

Tyler was trying to catch her eye, but she ignored him and hung her head. Bringing Chris up here, now—her soul was in turmoil.

Jacob's voice broke. "My wife was in the house that Bertoller bombed. The blast burned and maimed her, but she was still alive. I carried her out. Many of the refugees were fleeing together, but I would not go until I had tended her wounds, stopped the bleeding, held her in case she was going to die. I sat in the shadow of the burning house, listened to the police sirens coming, heard justice miscarrying even then, even in how they began the investigation. I knew they were against us and that we were the targets of something bigger than we dreamed. She clung to me, and I wept silently over her and told her, again and again, that it would be all right. It would be all right, for we were Oneness, and we were stronger than death and stronger than darkness. It would be all right, for we would triumph. The plans of the enemy would backfire. We would be seen to be victorious. And she would live."

Reese's eyes left the tombstone and fixed on his face. The pain there was as raw as it must have been twenty years ago— both the pain and the passion.

"She did live. Miraculously. I carried her away, keeping to the shadows, avoiding the creatures that hunted us. It wasn't only men, it was demons also; on our heels like slavering dogs. Sometimes in the form of slavering dogs. That night was the stuff of a thousand nightmares. But we survived it. We walked for days. I don't know how long. I only know that she was on the edge of death, and I was holding her here with everything in me. I walked until I was nearly faint with hunger and thirst, but I realized we could not keep going—she needed food and drink, and her pain was too bad . . . she was so badly burnt, so badly wounded."

Reese closed her eyes. She didn't want to think about it—didn't want to imagine the details of what that journey looked like.

His voice caught, choked up in his throat. "So I left her. I found a secluded place, where I thought she would be safe. I went into town to find something for us to eat."

His voice hardened. "When I came back, she was dead."

"I'm sorry," Reese said, but she wasn't sure the words were even audible.

"They had found her," Jacob stressed. "She would have made it. But they found her."

He cleared his throat. "After that I realized that we had not won—we had lost the battle. Everywhere I looked, there was nothing but loss. The Oneness was reeling. And I came to understand that something was out of balance. Blood had been shed, and it had to be avenged. But when I tried to talk to others in the Oneness about our duty to set things right, they refused to hear me."

Insects buzzing in the trees behind them were a morbid chorus to the story.

"I realized I had to do the work myself. I dug into what had happened, realized who was responsible—this man. I learned other things about him. His life was chaos. More than any senseless demon, he had chosen wickedness and walked it out faithfully. I knew he had to die. His blood for my wife's. His soul for the countless souls he had doomed and tortured. So I took a gun and I tracked him down. I made it past his bodyguards and security systems, and I stood facing him in his own bedroom and accused him of his crimes."

Reese was riveted. The story was supposed to end with Jacob getting his revenge—surely it had to end there. But it hadn't. The date on the gravestone told her that—Jacob had not shot him.

"You didn't do it," she said.

The grief on his face was hard to look at.

"I failed. I didn't have the courage. When it came to pulling the trigger, the weakness and compromise of the Oneness overcame me, and I walked away—and he laughed."

Jacob traced his fingers over the name etched in granite. "That was when I found my way here. I came for morbid reasons, I suppose. To dwell on my failure. To think about it. To try to find the truth. I knew he would die someday, and it had not been by my hand."

"But he did die someday," Reese said. "Justice was done."

His eyes flashed. "It was not. Not for a moment. He continued to ply his trade—gambling, drugs—for sixteen years. He destroyed countless more lives. I watched it happen. I even tried to get to him again, but I could never replicate my success of the first time. This gravestone is not a monument to justice, to our triumph. It is a monument to our failure. To our pathetic weakness."

He swept his arm out. "They all are. After my failure that day, I spent three years in this graveyard. I squatted in a shack on an old farm half a mile down the road. Came here every day, to think and to pray and to remember. Slept here on nights when it was warm and dry enough. I went into town and looked up all their names. I know every man and every woman here. I know all the evil they represent—and all of it unchecked, unavenged, unchallenged. Did the Oneness do a thing to alter the course of chaos in their lives? Oh, we stepped in here and there—tried to help someone. Got a child or two into our own ranks. But that's all. Compared to the lives they destroyed, we had no triumph at all. And all the time the balance is off. All the time evil goes on triumphing, and we go on letting it—and nothing is done, nothing balances the scales again, much less wins them."

His eyes were on fire. "Bertoller himself encountered the Oneness numerous times before the bombing, when he already had blood on his hands and they knew it. They never stopped him. Never brought about justice. The massacre was fitting, in a way. It was another monument to our failure."

Reese stared at the name on the grave, and it seemed to her that it was mocking them.

Jacob's voice quieted, calmed. "Finally, sure that I understood the truth, I went to begin my own cell. My own Oneness community. But they could not be weak like the rest. They could not fail as I had failed, as so many have failed. They could not lose sight of their purpose. So I determined to raise my community in two ways. They would know purity first—so they would love goodness, and innocence, and hate wickedness with all that was within them. They would be separated from the world, holy. And secondly they would know power and not be afraid to use it. You accuse me of consorting with evil, but I consort only with power. I raised a family of faithful ones, people with the clear eyes to see what is right and what is wrong. And they were ready to learn power, so I began to teach them. That is why I brought Clint into our midst—to teach us power. To teach us to harness it. He is brilliant, and gifted."

"He's evil."

"You say that not knowing anything about him. Do you think I would let him through my doors without knowing him first? I, who have shepherded my community so carefully for so many years?"

"That is hard to believe," Tyler said, and Reese couldn't tell if he was sincere or his words were sarcasm. Not that she could blame him. He had seen much too much of Clint.

Jacob was incredibly convincing.

But she remembered Julie and steeled herself.

"The problem is," she said, "you didn't bring your people into the Oneness at all. They don't know the Spirit. They only know your rules, your ways."

Jacob flushed. "I submit that one who has been an ardent member of the corruption that we now call Oneness for so long cannot clearly say what it is to know the Spirit or not."

She pictured him living here, a young man dwelling among tombs, for three years.

"You fixated on darkness for so long," she said. "How do

you know you can trust your knowledge?"

She turned her back and walked away through the grass, her eyes trailing the gravestones, every one calling up spectres of lives lived in lust and greed and damage, the picture Jacob had painted. She wished she could believe he was wrong about all these people.

But she didn't.

She'd seen too much in Lincoln, as part of the cell that was forever tracking and fighting the demonic, to question him much on that point. But it shook her now, to look back. Because they had always just gone after the demonic, and in all of her years that had never truly solved the problem. It was always people at the back of things. People using each other. People turning on each other. People destroying each other.

And it was people they never really stopped.

People the Oneness only tried to help, to serve, to save.

What if Jacob was right?

What if you couldn't win the battle that way?

What if some people simply had to be stopped, taken out of the way, so that they could not live ninety-eight years of darkness worse than demons?

What if, instead of using their swords to make a real difference, they had been play-fighting on the field of the world all these years?

And what if he was right about her—and years of closing her ears and eyes to the truth had warped everything she thought she knew, so much that she could not trust herself to know anything?

Tyler appeared beside her.

"You're letting him get to you."

"He's . . ."

"He's not right."

She stopped. "He could be."

"Reese, he's not. I'm new to the Oneness. I haven't been ignoring any 'truth' for years and years. And I know the Oneness is good, and Clint is evil—the demons are evil, Clint's power is evil. What you do, what all of you do, is good and right."

She looked around the graveyard, its neat, silent stones monuments to something. Jacob was waiting by the giant head-stone of Bertoller, keeping his distance, letting them talk. She imagined him again a young man, thrashing out his questions and his grief among the dead. He was mad. Or a prophet.

And she thought of Chris.

"We let his wife die," she whispered.

"But you didn't let me die. Or Chris. You saved Chris, Reese." He hesitated. "Besides, I don't think you can blame yourselves for what happened to his wife. Bertoller did that."

"And we didn't stop him."

"It's not your job to stop him."

"It's our job to combat corruption. It's our job to hold things in order, to hold them together. It's our job to keep the world safe in the hands of love, to be the hands of love. Are we doing that if we let men like that go unopposed?"

Tyler didn't answer. He looked confused and lost.

"I'm sorry," she said. "I know these are heavy questions. Honestly, I've never asked them before. You're right. He's getting to me."

She lowered her voice and scuffed the ground. "Maybe that's a good thing."

Tyler looked back at him and squinted, as though he was trying to see the man more clearly. Then, unexpectedly, he said, "He was right about one thing for sure."

Reese raised her eyebrows. "And that is?"

"You and Chris. I think you're meant to be together. He really loves you. You love him too. But not before he's Oneness. Jacob is right about that."

She just stared at him.

He looked down and shuffled his feet in the dirt. "I'm sorry," he said, but he wasn't.

He wasn't sorry at all, and she didn't want him to be.

"No," she said. "You're a good friend." She turned to look at Jacob again. "I don't know what to do about him. I'm supposed to be bringing him back into the fold so he won't be a threat to the Oneness anymore. I'm doing a terrible job."

"Well, ball's in your court now. Right? You're taking turns. So you take him somewhere."

"Where? I can't compete with this!"

"Because you don't believe in what you're saying," Tyler said, "so you can't think of anything to support you. Jacob believes in himself so much he'll find proof of his beliefs everywhere." Tyler looked at her with an expression between a command and a half-questioning suggestion. "Maybe you need to figure out what you really believe, instead of just trying to figure out what he does."

She found it in her to grin. "When did you get so smart?"

He shrugged. "Dunno. Just born that way, I guess."

She swatted him, leaning hard on her crutches to give herself a free hand, and he ducked and laughed. "Maybe you're right. But this was not the plan."

"Plans come from the Spirit, right? Is the Spirit usually predictable?"

"I meant my plan."

"Maybe that's the problem."

"Tyler . . ."

"Yes?"

Standing among the gravestones, with his sneakers scuffed and his hair in a long tangle as usual, he looked like a little boy. And she wanted to smack him and hug him at the same time.

"Thanks for being so difficult. I think I need you right now."

"No problem," he said.

And together, their eyes strayed back to Jacob.

He had left the huge gravestone and was wandering, reading the smaller stones, reviewing all he knew about these people.

His failures.

His vision for the future.

Reese realized she'd been waiting for him to take control again, to tell them it was time to go and move on to the next place. But it was her turn. Technically, she was in control now.

Even though she felt a lot like the world had turned upside down.

"Well," she said faintly, "I guess it's time to go."

"What are we going to do?"

"What you said," she answered. "Figure out what I believe. Figure out whose side I'm on." She flashed him a tired smile. "There's no point in continuing all this if I don't know that."

She motioned to Jacob when he looked their way and headed back toward the car, feeling heavier on her crutches than she had when they'd arrived.

Heavier in her heart, in her mind.

She knew what she didn't say.

If Jacob was right, and she accepted his beliefs as true, she was exiling herself again—cutting herself off from everything and everyone she loved.

Choosing it this time.

But if she had learned anything from what David had done to her, it was that truth mattered.

\* \* \* \* \*

Mary's hand shook as she reached for David's. His eyes were trained on hers, in hers, riveting, compelling.

He was a liar, a practiced liar, yet she hoped to find truth by entering into his soul.

This was madness.

And yet she had no other choice.

Truth about him—worse, truth about herself.

It was she, he insisted, who had sent him down this path years ago. She who had twisted him, perverted him, turned him against the Oneness. She who had done to him what he was trying to do to others.

Two things, she feared.

One was this power. Yes, Oneness could do this. Yes, they could enter each other's hearts to this degree. Yes, they could go past all the normal boundaries of human knowledge, all the normal limitations. They did not do it. Not because it was morally wrong, but because it cost.

It cost to enter so fully into what they were.

And a voice whispered to her:

If you are afraid of the cost, you will never enter the fullness of what you are or of what I am.

The second thing she feared: that she would see herself through David's eyes and know herself to be the enemy of all she truly loved, to know herself a hypocrite, to know herself a darkness greater than any she had tried to fight.

Since she was a teenager, Oneness had been Mary's life.

She had given herself to it, served it, proselytized for it. It was her family, her passion, her work, and her heart.

She feared discovering that from some deeper place within her, she had been working to undo what she loved so much.

That her whole life would prove to be a sham.

A desperate bid to convince herself she meant something and lived for something beyond herself without uncovering the truth.

Behind her, April and Chris were talking, their voices a low murmur under the sound of the waves, the boat kicking up spray, the sail flapping, the birds calling.

Before her, David's eyes drew her in.

He took her hand—she had not found the courage to take his.

He closed his eyes.

And she closed hers, knowing that in that moment she was stepping outside of the world where the sun was, where the waves were, where her family was. And she was stepping into a man's soul.

The first thing she knew was darkness.

Darkness washed over her, but not the darkness of fear. This was the darkness of a womb, of a deep, quiet, sacred place where life was formed.

Silence here was a heavy hush, a brooding.

Then a rush of thought, emotion, and being—like a freight train bearing down on her, screaming over and through her, overwhelming.

She gasped and woke up.

She was in a place she recognized. A house. She couldn't remember why she knew it, or what had happened here—only that in some sense she belonged in this place. She looked down to see where she was sitting and found that she could not see herself.

Nor could she see David. She was not looking through his eyes. But he was there—a presence she could feel, but as invisible to her as she was herself.

He was younger here.

This was a long time ago.

Twenty years ago.

That should mean something to her, but in this moment, here, it didn't.

She had a sense that she was to wait, and to watch, as much outside of herself as she could be. And so, very conscious that she was doing it, she quieted the voice of her own mind and sank back into his.

She became nothing.

Or nearly nothing.

It was impossible, she found, to be rid of herself completely.

Someone in the room was talking. The conversation was nothing of consequence—so little so that she drifted out of it without really taking in what was being said, distracted by other details. It was night, and an open window was letting a cool breeze through ruffled curtains. The occasional car passed on the street outside, and the distant thumping of a stereo added its rhythm to the night, but it was late fall and the neighbourhood was indoors—cozy behind closed doors. Here, the sense was overwhelmingly one of comfort, of home. Of fellowship and connection, belonging.

It was Oneness at its best, warming her heart, enveloping her. Oneness giving even the shabby decorating of the house—a large house she thought, having a sense of space beyond this sitting room—a meaning and glow beyond themselves.

Someone walked into the room, and she turned to look at him, and felt her own heart lurch.

Hers, not David's. Her heart asserting itself because this face, this young man, meant so much to her.

Her brother.

Her twin brother.

He was cradling a child, a three-year-old who was half asleep snuggled against his chest. Like hers, Sam's build was slight, but he was strong, and more than a head taller than she was.

The bond with his spirit was as strong, as vital, as she remembered it being. She realized she had known he was there even before he entered the room. They exchanged a glance now and smiled without words.

Exchanged a glance?

Yes, she was there too—in a corner of the room that she could not see, physically there, her younger self.

But she wasn't in that self now. She was in David, seeing—to some extent—from his perspective.

She was supposed to be learning, so she wrested her attention away from Sam—oh, how she wanted to leave it there!—and tried to divine how David felt about her presence in this place twenty years ago. If he already viewed her as an enemy, or if—

Her attempt was thwarted by the blast.

She remembered this.

It all played out like she remembered it. It was the back of the house that blew off, killing everyone who was there, sending off a blast of heat that ripped through now and burned them all as they stumbled out the doors, coughing and choking in air that had been cool, had been moving lace curtains, and now was a black inferno.

The house was big—bigger than the impression she'd had standing in the sitting room. Big enough that nearly as many people managed to get out before the rest of the house blew as had died in the initial bombing.

Fear rose up and choked her, more blinding than grief, and she didn't know if it was hers or David's. But she saw Sam stumbling out, with his child in his arms, and the rest of the family—his wife and two other children—running to him from another door where they had escaped. And then they all joined hands and ran.

Ran from the second blast.

The second crippling, burning wave of heat.

She'd never forgotten the cries of those who didn't get far enough away.

She opened her eyes and was back on the boat. She looked across at David—somehow they were both lying on their backs now, side by side, with the spray stinging their eyes.

Her eyes were full of tears.

His were not. But she saw the pain in them anyway.

"These are my memories too," she said, licking her lips as though they were still burned, cracked and bleeding. "You weren't the only one who suffered. Who lost."

Sam. Now the grief rose up—sharp as it had been the first day after he was killed by the drug-addled teens who came so much later, when it should have been all over but wasn't.

She had never stopped grieving his lost, but somehow the pain had been buried under the years, matted down by time and other concerns and the company of others she loved.

It was not buried now.

She cried, tears just running down her face, pain too deep for sobs.

If anything, David looked satisfied.

But she hurt too badly, in this moment, with the smells and sounds of that night so fresh, to hate him for it.

"We aren't done," he croaked.

The memories weren't easy for him either.

She closed her eyes again.

Again the womb-like darkness, the rush of personality and feeling, and then she opened her eyes and they were in the country, twigs and dried grass snapping under their feet, mud sucking at them, insects biting. There were people before and people behind, urging children on, comforting each other. There was pain—the burns from the blast, the burning lungs from breathing it in and then running, and not stopping, convinced that they were running from something more terrible than a fire. More diabolical than a freak accident, a gas line blowing, whatever else the media might call it.

Hell was on their heels, and they knew it.

She recognized that Sam and his children were in this group, that these were still her memories. She had fled down this road, in this hour, under this moon. She had fled with this conviction of being hunted.

Which meant that David had been there too, right alongside her, the whole time.

And yet she had not remembered him.

The split presence—that this was both her memory and his—made it hard to stay tapped into him, to let herself relax into his personality and quiet her own thoughts.

Once again, she took herself in hand and ordered her own mind, her own heart, to quiet. It was harder this time. Knowing that Sam was here made her want to stay present.

But she did what she had to do.

This time she felt the throbbing confusion and heartache. The question drumming through David's veins with every step, every tortured breath.

Why?

Why?

Why?

And she felt his terrible grief, grief that was still partially numb but was fighting for his attention, threatening to overwhelm him, stop in his tracks, throw him into a ditch to stay there and weep and die.

Unlike her, he had lost someone he was especially close to in that blast.

Not just close to . . .

She heard the cry of his heart:

My baby!

She opened her eyes again. Back to the yacht. Back to the sun and the salt air, and the ropes overhead and the great white sail.

"You lost a child," she said. "You're a father."

"A real one," he said bitterly. "Not just some house parent."

But this time, as she stared into his eyes she didn't see the pain that had been there before. This, he had walled off. This, he would not go back to. And she thought, maybe, the bitterness was a wall. A protection he had built just so he would never have to face that pain again.

"Are you inventing theories?" he asked. "Trying to understand my pain so you'll know why I turned? You know nothing. I didn't turn against the Oneness for costing me my daughter. I believed your propaganda—that death was nothing, that we'd still be One, that she would be there on the other side. Death did not sting that day like it should have."

"It stung enough. I felt it."

"I was a man," he said. "I had a heart."

"You still are. You still do."

He closed his eyes. She realized he was weak—and so was she. This connection, this depth of being One, was costing them both.

She wondered why exactly he wanted it.

Why he was so open.

"No," he said, "I do not. I exorcised my heart a long time ago. If you see pain in my eyes, it is only because a man does not need a heart to feel pain. A man is an animal, and he can be tormented and whimper like one."

She closed her eyes too.

"I'm sorry for you."

"You shouldn't be. I am going to wreck you before this is over. You are going to hate me."

"That won't happen."

They were in a field, surrounded by shadows—a cornfield. Sam had lit a fire. His family and others were crowded around it, but David sat back, away, in the darkness, his soul twisting and gnawing with grief. And with guilt.

His baby.

His little girl.

She had been in the back part of the house, asleep.

He could not have saved her.

But he should have, he told himself, he should have run into the flames and tried. Or died.

But the Spirit had kept him alive. This was an election. A predetermined fate. As was hers. There was a reason. A plan.

Yet his soul still twisted, still churned. He did not cry but writhed in the darkness.

And Mary, facing her own grief and fear of twenty years ago again, found it easier to let go and lose herself in his pain.

Just before her own mind faded completely into his, she heard a voice somewhere, speaking it seemed from the moonlit sky above.

But no, that wasn't right. The voice was from another place.

April.

Saying, "What is that?"

**Richard stationed himself** in the parking garage where he could watch the elevator that led to her apartment, and, bored after a while—and concerned that he would miss something—he created a circuit for himself, stalking from the garage to the street outside where he could scan comers on all sides to the lobby where he could watch who went up, and back to the parking garage. A doorman questioned him and he told them he was working for Melissa. She confirmed it when the doorman called.

For which he was grateful.

His own restlessness and pacing reminded him of April, who tended to run when she wanted to work something out. His usual tendency was exactly the opposite: to sit, to find a quiet place, to sink deeply into prayer and be caught up in the rush of Spirit, there to forget himself, to almost leave his body, to transcend.

He felt he ought to do that now, but for some reason he could not quiet himself.

He couldn't shake the sense of guilt over having cut Melissa off from her healing.

He knew, even as he admitted that to himself, that he was thinking foolishness. The hive, the children, the demonic powers that had controlled them—they were not trying to help Melissa. Even if they had the capability of holding the cancer at bay, even if they could cheat death for a time and help her cheat it, they were doing nothing for her good. All was a plot, all a scheme to destroy her along with everyone else.

And yet when he searched his heart, he found that he could not blame her questions or her choices. She was right. He had been asked to die, but only in battle, only knowing he was a victor. He had never been asked to face what she was facing, or to justify it to himself: to explain why the Oneness, the source of all true life, could not stop death from eating away at his body and truncating a gift and calling greater than most would ever know.

It didn't make sense.

He also confessed, as he paced the sidewalk outside the building and then scanned the lobby for what seemed like the hundredth time before taking the elevator to the parking garage yet again, that he cared about this girl more than he had cared about anyone in a long, long time.

Oneness was a strange thing. It bound all together in a single body, but some would always be closer than others. There were those who were close by proximity and common calling—like Mary. He and she were like two fingers on the same hand, always about the same work, deeply connected and believing in one another almost more than they believed in the greater ideal of the Oneness. It was that way because it had to be; the Oneness was infinite but every member finite; they could only be close, functionally close, to so many.

Others were close because of how their personalities meshed or because of a history together.

Melissa was something different.

He knew as he walked his circuit that if he found anyone threatening her, he would die to keep her safe and count it nothing.

He could not put a name to it. He asked himself if this was romantic love—if, after all, he might become one of the few Oneness who married. But it was not. It was something more stable, more deep even than that.

He could only describe it to himself as calling.

He was meant to love her. He was meant to keep her safe. She was meant to be a part of him like a strand of his own DNA.

He realized, with a sudden understanding that literally shook him where he stood, that he could not stand the idea of losing her.

She could not die.

It was unthinkable.

But you're asking her to, a voice said. That's what you want. For her to give up all ties to the powers that are keeping her alive and choose to die instead, just to prove that you are right.

Just to comfort you in your own convictions.

Your own conceits.

He stopped and buried his face in his hands, forcing himself to breathe, to seek, to calm.

To pray.

Spirit, he breathed. Spirit.

It was like calling into a well. Nothing answered but the echo of his own voice, yet he felt a sense of depth—perhaps a far distant stirring.

I have never doubted you, he prayed. I have never doubted. Not until now. Help me.

He lifted his eyes at the sound of the elevator doors opening, and there she was.

He was in the parking garage, and she got off the elevator with a sort of awkward grace, holding out her hand to him. Gone were the evening gown and the high heels. She wore a flowing skirt and a sleeveless shirt, casual but beautiful.

"The doorman told me you were stalking around like a . . . well, like a stalker. You told him you were working for me?"

"I am working for you."

She smiled, and it creased the corners of her eyes. "I know. I thought, since you are getting a workout pacing all over the place, I should feed you dinner."

"How did you know I was still pacing?"

"I called downstairs and asked."

He smiled. Now that she mentioned it, he was hungry.

And glad to be back in her presence.

They rode the elevator in companionable silence. She gave him another smile just before it dinged and the doors opened to the penthouse.

The smile vanished two seconds after they stepped out.

"What are you doing here?" she said. "Who are you?"

A smiling, well-dressed young man with a square jaw and blond hair rose from her couch. His accent, faintly European, set off every last alarm bell Richard had.

"Oh, you don't mind," he said. "I came to enjoy dinner with you both. And to help you."

"You didn't answer the lady's questions, Clint," Richard said. "Who are you, and what are you doing here?"

Movement from the kitchen momentarily distracted him, and he caught sight of black clothing and a smirking expression.

Alex.

"You know who I am," Clint said. "You both do. As far as what we are doing here—well, you might say we are closing a net."

* * * * *

There was a storm coming.

Tony could see it from the ridge behind the cottage. It was massing in the sky over the water, dark clouds hovering low and menacing. A breeze, deliciously cool but somehow threatening, was blowing straight at the land.

"Tony."

Angelica's voice was sharp. He turned. "What?"

"Jordan's gone."

His heart sank. "What?"

"He's gone. I could have sworn he was there a few minutes ago, but he's gone now and I can't find a trace of him."

"Get everybody searching."

"Spread them out? Are you sure that's smart?"

He knew what she was asking.

He felt it too.

There was an attack coming.

No, they couldn't spread everyone out. Not even to find Jordan. They had to get them safely clustered in the cottage, where the shield was strongest, where they could be best defended.

He wished Richard was here.

He turned and eyed the coming storm again. He thought he could see creatures in the clouds, wings and eyes, armour and swords.

He was imagining that.

It was just a storm.

But an attack was coming.

"Get everyone inside," he said, changing tacks in a moment. "Be ready—for anything. I'm going after Jordan. If I can't find him and we run out of time, I'll come to join you."

And we run out of time.

They both knew what he meant by that.

She nodded, drew her sword—out of thin air, it looked like, but Tony could feel his forming in his hand too, whether in response to the demons quickly arriving or just to his own anxiety, he couldn't say. She rushed off toward the cottage, calling for Susan Brown. Enlisting help in getting all of the kids back.

Thunder rumbled, and Tony turned back to the cliffs.

Jordan, he thought, would have gone in one of two directions:

Down the road, back toward civilization.

Or down the cliffs.

Both away from the shield.

He had no idea which way to check. He closed his eyes and tried to pray, not his strong point in the spiritual disciplines of life in the Oneness, but one that came naturally in a situation like this—a plea, a desperate call for insight.

He didn't know whether he was answered, but he felt drawn toward the cliffs.

He started on the path he and Jordan had explored earlier that day, the storm before him in a vista of dark grey and gathering electricity, gathering thunder. He was plunging into that looming threat.

Going demon hunting.

No, he told himself, going boy hunting.

But he feared he would find both at once. Both together. And both needing to be fought.

Reese, Mary, Richard, he thought. Wherever you are, whatever's going on, hurry.

We need to win this fight.

And we need to win it fast.

* * * * *

The storm had blown up fast—too fast, unnaturally fast. April watched it come, letting the sword form in her hand. Chris was taking in the sails, and he called on his mother to give him a hand.

Diane cast a pointed look at Mary and David as she appeared from the hatch. "So they did it?"

The two were stretched out side by side, eyes closed, looking as though they were asleep.

Or dead.

"I don't know what they're doing," Chris said, testy, "but I hope they hurry up and finish, because what's coming I can't fight."

April's eyes were fixed on the gathering clouds. A bolt of lightning broke through the grey, momentarily slashing silver over the dark sky.

Diane, coming up beside her as she followed Chris's instructions, leaned closer to her and followed her gaze to the clouds.

"It's not natural, is it?" she asked.

"No. I don't think so."

"Can you see demons?"

"I can feel them."

Diane sighed and flexed her hand. "So can I."

April cast her a compassionate glance. "Best just to let it

form. You don't want to be caught without defense. And I think they may attack very quickly."

Diane went back to her work, head bowed until April said a sharp, "There."

She looked up and saw them too: the edges of wings in the clouds, the leer of eyes. They were forming as they had in the warehouse: a core, without bodies or need of them. It wasn't common for such a gathering to be able to form so far away from land. They needed something to feed off of, something from which to draw energy and form. When they had a source, a core attack was powerful. The demons weren't limited by bodies or able to be cast out.

"What are they drawing from?"

"Maybe David."

Diane cast another almost panicked look at the two lying on the deck, lost in some inner world.

They had come out here to convert him or kill him.

They hadn't really asked what would happen if they ran out of time.

* * * * *

Deep in the past, David was still wracked with pain and guilt over losing his child—and still believing, fervently, almost blindly, in the Oneness. That the Oneness gave meaning not just to his life but to his loss. That the Oneness would make it all worth it in the end. That the Oneness meant he could transcend all this—the burns, the pain, the heartbreak.

The hunting.

Mary, deep in David's soul, felt it all and knew her own heart, somewhere far away, was breaking.

Her own heart, somewhere far away, knew what he would become. She didn't know why. Only that he told her it was her fault.

Pushing through the heartbreak, trying to stay with him and not withdraw in her own sense of pending loss and grief and guilt, she found another one: a heartbreak mingled with joy. Sam was here. Sam and his children and his wife. Her twin, her family.

She had forgotten how much she missed them all. Time had dulled it. But they were here, sitting around their little campfire in the cornfield, huddled around the burning husks, whispering and comforting each other and her.

She still could not see herself, but she still knew she was present. She knew that her niece was curled up in her lap, snuggling against her, and that Sam often turned to her and whispered something that brought her strength.

There were others with them as well. Others came throughout the night, pulled by the magnetism of Oneness to the hidden place in the cornfield. The group grew, all united and yet separated in their various griefs, so that Mary felt she was justified a little in having forgotten David's presence that night. The details of who and where and when had blurred in the smoke and the darkness of the night.

Sam spoke to them all, the whole group in their woundedness. He reminded them of what they were: servants of mankind, expressions of the Spirit, keepers of the world. He told them that darkness would not triumph though it tried with all its fury.

They had only just begun to sleep, to calm enough to really rest, when a teenager broke into the clearing, gasping, his sides heaving from a long and desperate run.

"They're coming," he choked out.

No one asked precisely who—or what.

They simply pulled themselves up and kept going.

And David, denied the opportunity to truly sink and grieve, felt as he ran the first glimmerings of real despair.

Perhaps it was the juxtaposition—Sam's words of encouragement and victory followed so quickly by the news that they were still being hunted. That it wasn't over with the blast and the incalculable losses. That more loss was coming.

It got harder as they went. Somewhere along the line, he had been injured—he couldn't remember where. Perhaps back at the house, perhaps while fleeing down the country roads. His ankle was swelling and getting harder to walk on. The group began to pull ahead of him, farther and farther, he and a few others who lagged. The part of his consciousness that was Mary didn't know them, but David evidently did.

They drew back and finally veered away in a different direction.

"We might as well split up," one of them said. "Give the demons a split target to follow."

They knew, when they said that, that they might give their lives so the others could get away.

They believed in that kind of sacrifice.

David believed in it.

The main road was leading through cornfields. A farm road, it was dirt and gravel, uneven and full of potholes. They chose to veer away to the right, hoping to make it back to a clearer, paved public road. As much as that might make them easier targets to find, it would also help with injuries—David wasn't the only one limping on a bad leg at this point—and get them closer to potential help if something did happen.

The plan failed. At first the road did hit pavement, giving them hope, but after some time of stumbling through the dark, it turned into a narrow, ridged dirt road that plunged into the woods.

They kept going. They didn't know what else to do. They paused once, wanting to discuss it, but for all of them the sense of something on their heels was so strong that it pushed them back into motion.

Any hopes that the trees were just a small stand, something they would be out of in minutes, died away as the woods got thicker, the moon disappeared completely behind tangled branches and the remaining leaves of fall, and the sounds of autumn insects droned louder.

Soon they were stumbling through total darkness.

David's ankle twisted and gave out. He sprawled on the ground, too exhausted even to cry for help.

Someone noticed anyway. There were four of them in the splinter group. One turned back, a young woman. Tried to help him up.

He was too tired, too hurt.

"Just leave me here," he rasped.

He didn't know if they would have.

At that moment the sense of being hunted shifted:

To a sense of being surrounded.

There was nowhere left to run.

It wasn't just dark now; it had turned thick—like the air was made of tar, too thick to breathe, too thick to move in. David could not get up, could not move. Pressure on his chest grew until he thought it would burst.

He tried to move his arms, to push himself up, but it seemed as though they had sunken into the earth, and the earth itself was holding them in a vice.

From the trees directly in front of him, he heard a laugh.

A young man stepped out of the darkness. How they could see him, David didn't really know. There was no light—nothing to illuminate him. Yet he was clearly visible, dark on dark.

He looked perhaps college age. Blond hair, a strong jaw, clothing that would have fit in at an elite prep school.

He spoke with a faintly European accent.

"You have come so far," he said. "You did not really think running would do you any good?"

He heard someone else answering but could not make out words. The tone was brave. Valour, like the martyrs of old.

The response running through David's own mind was different.

First, confusion—and, incongruously, curiosity.

"Who are you?"

He had expected—he didn't know what. Demons, in their own forms, emboldened and empowered by the blast. Perhaps the angry, drug-empowered members of a gang or some criminal with revenge on his mind—whoever had bombed the house.

Not this.

This young man was something completely different. Possessed, yes—but David had seen that before. This was a level of power and possession in a human form he had never encountered, or even really imagined.

The way the air felt, the way the earth had become a chain, shackles around his wrists, keeping him down, the sense of being surrounded—it all came from this young man as surely as it did from the demonic powers within him.

This evil was human.

Deep within David's pysche, Mary struggled against what she was seeing.

It was Clint, in the darkness of that wood.

Clint, not a day younger than he was now—twenty years later.

Clint, who David had somehow sought out again and forged an allegiance with. Or perhaps it was the other way around.

He had been there. He had been part of the attack that changed all their lives. And yet David blamed her, and not Clint, for his suffering.

She didn't understand.

Her own wrestling was distracting her from what was still happening—still playing out in that wood as if it were today, as if it had played out perpetually every day since. As though moments did not pass, time did not pass, but simply became films that never ceased to play on a screen of their own.

They were talking. More bravado from some of the others. Mocking, cynical laughter, from Clint.

Then he killed them.

All except David.

David he left lying on the ground with his ankle throbbing and his heart shattered.

He stepped directly in front of him, so that David was staring at his feet, and crouched down. He picked up a handful of dirt and blew it into David's face.

"And this is all you are," he said. "Dust. And I, not you, control dust. In Oneness, you are trying to transcend earth, and you never will. You never can become more than what you are. Handfuls of dirt in the universe, going back to dirt in the end."

He turned and walked away, slapping his hands together to clean them of the dirt, and David wept out the grit in his eyes.

The bodies of his friends lay around the clearing, and he could not see them to avoid them in the moonless forest. When at last he could motivate himself to move again—as much to crawl away from the horror as to try to get anywhere else—he moved inch by inch, desperately hoping not to stumble across a corpse in the dark.

He couldn't handle that.

Clint's words haunted him.

Was he truly more than dust?

Was his daughter more than ashes?

Whether he was hurt worse than he knew, or whether the dirt blown into his face had effects he did not know about, he found as he crawled and stumbled through the rest of that night that his mind was twisted, exulted, depressed—wrung out—with thoughts that haunted, excited, and fascinated him: madness perhaps, delirium, or the attempt of a mind to escape from grief that was simply too great to carry. He found in himself a fatalism that was attractive: a desire to believe the witchcraft-worker in the woods, that he was only dust. For if he was only dust, if they all were only dust, than all that had happened was painful—but it did not mean much, in the end.

And death would end the pain.

There was freedom in the thought.

A freedom directly opposed to that offered by the Oneness.

But after all, the freedom of the Oneness was not freedom to escape or freedom to mean little. It was responsibility, terrible, heavy. It was servanthood, a yoke. It was meaning so great it was crushing.

Or so it felt to David, weary beyond life in the darkness of night, in pain and staggering toward some shelter or hope he could not see.

He wondered if the others had made it to safety somewhere.

We did, Mary wanted to tell him. We got away. Maybe you did save us, you and the others, by drawing them off.

Her own memories tried to filter into the scene. We crossed a lot of miles. Walked until we wanted to die. And then split up, like you did, for the same reason. We, me and Sam and his family found shelter with Douglas and Diane in the fishing village.

Now, looking back, she almost felt shame at how much more quickly she had found comfort, shelter, and relief. That while David wrestled with the very core of who he was, while he lost the last few shreds of companionship he had left, she was settling into a place she would call home and bringing others into the Oneness, creating a new family even as she was on the cusp of losing the old.

He didn't know when he broke out of the woods, only that eventually the sun was coming up over undeveloped rural land, highlighting fields of weeds and scrub. He found a padlocked trailer and tried to break in, but he didn't have the strength. Crawling into an open space beneath it, he fell asleep.

Fever.

What might have been days of fever.

Mary, both within him and without him, writhed in the throes of the illness herself even as she wanted nothing more than to run to him.

She hadn't known what he was going through.

Truthfully, she hadn't thought about him.

She remembered, in those days, an overwhelming sense of sickness, woundedness, and loss. So many of the Oneness had been scattered and were wandering the roads as hunted refugees. By this time the police had come out as against them, and those members who had remained in the city were being detained and questioned, and it was already fairly clear that false charges would win the day. They were still discovering how many had died.

Never had chaos seemed so strong and so prevalent, and they all felt it. In fact, the sense was so strong that Mary remembered throwing up intentional blocks: taking steps to close herself off mentally and emotionally.

She had never done that before or since, but it was too much. They all did it. No one could have functioned, could have saved themselves or anyone else, if they hadn't.

And even now, she knew it was irrational to think that she could have or should have done something different.

But she wished with all her heart that she had.

That she had stayed sensitive enough to know that someone was lost, was sleeping out under a trailer, equally wracked by fever and by doubt.

He probably wasn't the only one, she told herself.

We all suffered then.

Now, though, One with David's soul and experiencing his trials herself, his suffering seemed all that mattered in the world.

And if she had known where it would lead?

The damage it would do to him, the damage it would threaten to do to the Oneness?

She could not parse the timeline. She didn't know where she was while David was under the trailer on some forsaken piece of land. If she was still fleeing, still hiding, or if she was sitting warmly in Douglas's living room, telling his wife about the wonders of the Oneness.

Trying, maybe, to convince herself. Back then, so much was shaking that any chance to grasp surety had to be taken.

Somewhere far off, torn between her own memories and growing sense of guilt and the fever and madness that were taking their toll on David, she thought she heard a voice she recognized.

Calling her name.

Who . . . ?

A woman?

* * * * *

"Mary!" April shouted again, her back to Mary and David, the demons coming against her in an onslaught more furious than she could have imagined. "Mary, wake up, we need you!"

She blinked away stinging tears of frustration.

Her calls were doing no good.

Diane was already down.

Chris had disappeared in a swarm he could not fight.

She could not do this alone.

They were going to lose.

Rain lashed the boat even as waves tossed it, and it was all April could do to keep her feet.

"Mary!" she screamed against the storm and the fight—like the name was a prayer, and an answer to it would save the day somehow.

"**It's ironic that you** should be here together," Clint said, eyeing Richard and Melissa with something like pleasure. "Did he tell you, my dear, what he has done to you?"

Melissa didn't take the bait. "Who are you? Why are you in my apartment?"

"I am not a stranger, if that's what you're implying," Clint said. "I know all about you and your affairs of late. The children come to you—do you know who sends them? Where they come from? They come from me. I send them to you faithfully. It is I who look out for your health and make sure that you are given life. It is I who saw the children's remarkable gifts and developed them to begin with."

Richard could not speak. He did not know what he feared more—that Melissa would believe Clint and side with him, or that Clint would tell her what he, Richard, had done.

It was fairly clear he planned to.

And she wouldn't understand—not the way she was now. Not with her desperation to hang on to life and the hope the children—the possessed children—had given her.

His fear came out as a threat, aimed at Clint.

"What are you doing here?" he growled. "Answer the lady."

"I've come to enlist your help," he said, pointedly answering Melissa and not even looking at Richard.

"My help with what?"

Her tone was shaken, but bold. Richard found himself admiring her all the more.

"Rescuing the children," Clint said.

"Rescuing them? From what?"

"They are being held hostage." Now his eyes shifted, pinned Richard like an insect. "By this man and his cohorts." His voice lowered, playing deliciously off the reaction he saw in her eyes. "Oh, yes. Did he say he'd come to help you? To be your friend? He has come to make sure you die instead of living. He cannot bear that you should live, for it would alter his understanding of the world too terribly, and his understanding is more precious to him than any human being, not least you. Isn't that right, my friend?"

"We are not friends," Richard said.

It was all he could find to say.

He wanted to pour out his heart to Melissa—to explain everything, to apologize that he hadn't told her, to beg her to trust him anyway.

And to confess that he didn't really know how to answer

Clint's charge. That was why he hadn't told her all. Because he was going to ask her to die.

And he couldn't stand that.

"You're a liar," he growled.

Clint was nothing but smug. "Then explain where the children are. And under what conditions."

Richard's mouth hung, and Melissa turned to him. "Richard, please explain what he's talking about."

He heard the underlying plea.

Please prove that I can trust you.

Please prove that you are on my side and this man is not.

He wished he could prove that.

"They're in a cottage," Richard said.

"With whom?"

"With some of the Oneness."

"Under armed guard."

"Only armed with the Spirit sword. We all carry them, all the time. Even she does."

"And under what else?" He looked more smug, more pleased, than ever.

"Under a shield," Richard admitted.

Melissa sat down. Her face had gone grey.

"Better than that," Clint said. "It's not as though they're under a shield to keep their demons depressed, hmmm? When I say 'demon,' let us all think of the same thing: not of evil, but of power, of gifts. Mankind has often used the term that way, have they not? To describe the gifts, the sensitivities, the perspectives that sometimes drove them mad in pursuit of artistic vision, purity, love. It is the true sense of the word. You have personified them as something inherently evil only because you need an enemy to fight, and you are afraid of man ever becoming all he should be—free, and not bound by your chains of sameness and responsibility to a mass."

"I call them what I call them," Richard said, "because I've seen their eyes, and their wings, and heard their voices, and nearly been killed by them. And my good friends, and my family, have nearly been killed by them."

"Because you set yourselves up as their enemies right out of the gate," Clint said. "What do you expect them to do? Yes, you've been attacked by demons. And Melissa has been healed by them."

He turned to her, his presence courtly, beseeching. The voice of confident reason and mastery. "The fact is, my dear, the children are only 'possessed' by their own higher angels, their own true selves. You've seen that for yourself. But what I have tried to train, encourage, and develop, this man has done all in his power to destroy."

He turned back to Richard. "Come, now. Explain it. Tell her what exactly you've done to the children, and why you're keeping them under a shield. What you're afraid is going to happen."

He looked at Melissa. Blue eyes looked back at his, pleading.

"Richard. Please."

All the strength wanted to go out of his legs. He wanted to sit down, bury his face in his hands. But Clint was here, and he could not be so weak in the presence of his own enemy.

No matter how silver-tongued, how beguiling that enemy could be.

"We freed them," he said. His voice was threatening to break, to shake, but he wrestled it under control.

"You what?"

"Melissa, please, listen to me, and trust me. This man, no matter what he says, is my enemy and yours. He's the enemy of all Oneness and all that is good and whole in the world. He kidnapped and plotted to kill a number of our own, to burn them alive in a house full of leaking gas—was it your 'higher angel' that gave you that idea, Clint? Some of us tried to save them, and Clint used the children to incapacitate me. Their demons—not their 'power,' no matter what he says—threatened to kill them if I tried anything, and I couldn't just let that happen. So they held me helpless, hostage, for a little while. Held both my hands like little kids taking a walk in the park with their daddy. And I figured, if they'd been dealing with the likes of this snake all their lives, likely they needed a daddy. So I just held their hands tight back and loved them through that grip just as hard as I could, and by the time that fight was over, they got past their demons and cried out for freedom of their own accord, and Mary set them free." He faltered. "Mary. One of our own. A good woman."

Melissa looked stricken. He could only imagine what she was feeling—hers was a depth of emotion he could share, but she was walling him off. Probably walling them all off.

"So yes," he finished. "Yes, they're behind a shield. Yes, some of the Oneness are guarding them. It's for their own protection.

Because we figured this guy would come for them, and so would their demons."

"That's not the whole truth," Clint said.

He didn't seem one bit shaken, one bit thrown off, by anything Richard had said.

Like the truth didn't matter even the tiniest bit.

Like he knew the lie would conquer.

But he knew, now, the 'truth' Clint was fishing for.

And it was true. So he would speak it first, before this man could spin it.

"We are protecting them from themselves, yes," Richard said. "The chances are very good that if they do not join the Oneness, they will invite the demons back to take over again."

"And then they could heal me again," Melissa said.

Her words fell in the room like a sentence. And an accusation. All in one.

"Yes," Richard admitted.

"And right now, there is no one to heal me. In two days the children won't be here, and I will start to lose ground again."

"That is precisely what will happen," Clint said. His eyes gleamed. "But I think you do not imagine how fast you will lose that ground."

Richard wanted to kill him, then and there. He was threatening her. The bald-faced devil.

No, worse than the devil.

The man.

"That's why I'm here," Clint said softly. "I came to collect you so we can go together and collect the children."

"Why do you need her?" Richard asked, but Clint ignored him. Melissa didn't seem to have heard. She took the hand Clint was offering, hesitantly, and took a step toward the door.

And turned back and looked at Richard, who was still standing in the middle of the open seating area.

"What about him?" she asked.

"The clown?" Clint asked lightly. "I think he can wait here for you. Don't you? He wants to guard you. Let him do the next best thing and guard your home. Alex will help him."

She frowned. "He's a free man."

"No," Clint said gently, "he is not. Because I am not giving him his freedom just now."

She stopped and pulled her hand away. "Then I am not going with you."

This time, Clint did look surprised.

Richard was sure his face held the same expression.

"You brought a friend," Melissa said. "I want to bring one with me."

"I am your friend."

"No," she corrected him. "You are not. I'm not sure what you are, but you're not my friend . . . not anyone's friend, I don't think."

"I raised the children in their power."

"Then I'm sorry for them," she said.

And for a moment, something flashed across Clint's face that told Richard he knew he might actually lose her—that Melissa was not as securely in his grip as he thought.

Silently, inwardly, Richard cheered.

He had not known it until now either.

For a second confusion flashed across Clint's face, and then he turned to Alex and barked, "You come with us. Watch him."

He nailed Richard with his glare. "Come, then. I do not object to you seeing us get the children back—to you seeing how eagerly they come back, how much we do not even have to fight. Not like you are fighting for so many of yours, hmmm?"

"We would not have to fight for any of ours if you had not attacked us," Richard said.

Clint laughed. "So you say. But it is not I who am at the root of all your troubles. It is David. One of your own. He sought me out, asked for my help." He inclined his head in a mock bow. "I am only a servant."

Like everything the man said, the words felt a lie. Richard wanted to call them out, debunk them, expose them for the bald fabrication, the horrific twisting, they were.

But he couldn't, because this time Clint was right.

Speaking truth.

As almost impossible as that seemed.

Clint narrowed his eyes as he looked at Alex and Richard, from one to the other several times. He held his arm out to Melissa again, and she took it, but with her head held higher and her air more clearly watchful.

"You will come," Clint said to Richard. "Like she says. Come and see us get the children back. But if it should occur to you to try to stop me, or to attack our progress, I want you to stop and think about who else might be under my control just now."

Melissa did not react.

Somehow, he had cloaked his words so she could not hear them.

Falling in step behind them, Richard did all he could to send a subverbal message. Be careful.

And to his surprise, one came back: as clear as a word from the Spirit itself.

I will.

* * * * *

It was not David at the heart of the darkness threatening the Oneness.

Found under the trailer by a land surveyor days after he had collapsed there, a nearly dead David was airlifted from the remote location to a hospital in Lincoln, where Oneness found him and quickly took responsibility for his life. Once a regimen of IVs and pills had made him strong enough, they moved him to a safe house.

It took him a long time to want to do anything more than sleep. He lived in a half-coma, staying there intentionally because when he came out, he had to face all that had happened and all that had been thought, every alternative truth that had been entertained in his fearful and grieving and fever-destroyed mind.

And still there in the secret place of his soul, reliving it all, Mary struggled to patch together her own thoughts.

This was the chief: it wasn't him.

All this time, all this effort, all this recrimination, and it wasn't him after all.

They had gone after the wrong man.

Nor, as David had insisted, was she the real cause.

It had been Clint all the time.

Or, at least, the man who now went by that name.

Undoubtedly, many of David's actions had been evil. His intents had been evil. He had powered the core in the warehouse; he had exiled Reese; he had shot the hermit and gathered the hive. He was as given over to his bitterness and hate as any man had ever been, and in his own way was as far gone as the possessed man who pretended to be in his employ but was all the time directing every piece of the game according to his own master strategy.

David refused to wake up for nearly two years.

Something far away was calling for her, screaming for her. She was needed. Desperately needed. She tried to get back, but the lethargy, the coma of David's memories held her away from the voices calling.

On the yacht deck, David opened his eyes and smiled grimly.

He could not move.

He would not release himself that much, because to do so would be to release Mary as well.

And he was not ready to do that yet.

His hope, that he could draw her into his soul deeply enough to hold her captive there, was working.

The demons were swarming over the deck in nearly fully tangible form, stumping around like grasshoppers, like spiders, like horrors out of a children's fairy book of the old, Grimm kind.

Chris and Diane lay unconscious or dead on the deck.

April was still standing, only because the demons thought it enjoyable to toy with her.

David wanted to call out to them and tell them to stop it, because it could backfire to leave any one of them standing. He had seen that in too many encounters with them. To be one was to be One, with the strength of all, though they were likely not aware of that to any full extent.

He was glad the boy, Tyler, was not here. Somewhere he had discovered the truth of Oneness enough to escape paralysis. Better that he not be here to pass that understanding on.

He wished he had the strength to talk, that he could pull out of his soul sleep completely enough to address April.

So, he would tell her, we get to kill you after all. What is this, the third time? You would think your friends would take a hint and protect you better. That they would get some idea of how important, how key, you are to everything. But they don't. They just treat you like another common foot soldier, because that is how the Oneness is. No one better than another, no matter how naturally superior; no one allowed to rise above the mud.

That was why the Oneness would lose. Because they insisted on denying the truth about each other and about themselves.

Unexpectedly, he felt a twinge of conscience. His own journey had begun in the anger, grief, and doubt birthed through the cruel and unjust deaths of people like April.

His own daughter would have been just about her age.

He had come a long, long way.

But he closed his eyes again and refused to think any more about that.

* * * * *

"The parking garage is down," Richard said when Alex hit an elevator button going up.

"We're not taking the car," Clint answered.

"I have a perfectly good one waiting down there."

Clint ignored him.

Melissa offered Richard a halfhearted smile, meant to be encouraging, he thought. He was at least encouraged that she wasn't treating him like the enemy, even if she wasn't sure yet where she stood on everything she'd just learned.

The elevator took them up to a service floor just above the penthouse, one they weren't supposed to be able to access without a special key, but the doors opened seemingly at Clint's whim. From there they climbed a ladder to access the roof.

The city of Mark spread out below them and rose around them, lines of traffic, lights, glass and steel. The air was cooler up here instead of hotter: heat rose, but only heated its environs where it was trapped. Way up here, some thirty stories above street level, it dissipated into cooler, thinner air.

Clint strode to the parapet at the front of the building and stood atop it as though he would leap. Richard's heart went still for a moment at the thought that Clint was actually going to require them to jump and expect him to take care of them somehow.

He did not actually doubt that the man could do it.

He was just fairly sure Clint would conveniently forget to take care of him.

Clint spread out his arms, facing them, exultant master of space and air and time. "Come away with me, then," he said.

"I'm not going to jump," Richard said.

"Of course you're not." Fool, said his tone. "The way I travel requires no such theatrics. Only mastery. And thankfully for you, I have all the mastery any of us need."

Even as he spoke, the ground seemed to rush out from beneath Richard's feet. They were airborne—perhaps. He felt as though he could see the surface of the earth rushing beneath him, a blur: the steel and concrete of the city whisking past, the browns and greens of the countryside, the farm fields; the sweep of mountains, yellow and pine; the sea. He felt no wind, no sense of movement, only a profound displacement—as though if he tried to put his feet down somewhere he would fall forever, never able to recover his location in the world.

It stopped.

They were on a patch of wooded ground, tall pines on every side. Richard retched, only mildly comforted by the knowledge that Melissa and Alex were doing the same thing.

Clint sounded amused. "It takes only a little getting used to."

Alex said something mouthy, but Richard was still too sick to catch the words.

"You know," Clint said, "the sad thing is that you could do this too. Especially a man like you, a man of prayer and in tune with the Spirit. There is a great deal you are capable of that you have never even asked to explore. You are content to stay low, common, like the rest of your kind. But you are a man of far greater power and ability than even you have any idea. That is why you cannot defeat me. Because for all your vaunted talk of transcendence, and for all that I believe in nothing but myself and the dust, I have far more faith than you."

Clint stopped and arrested Richard with his eyes, ignoring the fact that Richard was still recovering from being sick. When he spoke, Richard knew he was cloaking again—that no one else could hear him.

"Mark my words," he said. "I have just said to you the truest thing I will ever say to you. I do not know why I said it. But I loathe the idea that any word I speak should be wasted."

Richard felt shaken.

Finished being ill, and with Clint no longer speaking to him, he took a moment to feel his feet solidly under him and become more aware of his surroundings. The smell of pine sap was strong in the air, but it didn't cover up the scent of salt, nor the distant sound of waves. The ground sloped sharply away to the west. Chances were they were near the cliffs.

And near the hermit's cottage.

Yes, this was Tempter's Mountain.

A crashing in the trees alerted Richard to someone or something coming. He raised his head with a sinking feeling.

The feeling was not amiss. The crashing revealed itself, with a stumble into the clearing, as Jordan.

"Well done," Clint said with a smile. "You have escaped the shield."

The boy didn't seem to notice the rest of them at first. "I think they're chasing me," he said. "Help me get my powers back!"

Then his eyes transferred to Melissa and widened, and from her to Richard—he ignored Alex completely.

"You!" he said.

"Yes, it's me," Richard said. "Think about what you're doing. Remember how you felt before we set you free. This is not a game, Jordan. You were a prisoner. You're going to go back to being a prisoner."

"You were powerful," Clint said. "And you want it back. You've had time to experience the 'freedom' these people promise you. Don't let them treat you like a stupid child."

"Jordan," Melissa said quietly, "I still need your help."

Richard closed his eyes.

That was the end of it.

And he couldn't—he couldn't watch the transformation.

He could feel the creatures as they gathered in the air, invisible presences all around, eager—hungry. He knew with his eyes closed that Jordan was thrilling to the presence, both excited and afraid, and that Clint was standing with his hands on the boy's shoulders, encouraging him to open himself up.

**Attack**          **203**

It wouldn't take much. Possession was always easier the second time.

Richard was vaguely aware of Alex at his elbow, guarding him, he supposed.

He wasn't sure why they felt that was necessary.

And then he heard a shout.

"Richard!"

The shout was happy, relieved. He knew the voice, young and optimistic: Tony had found them.

"Richard, stop them!"

He opened his eyes. Tony was still a ways away, running full-tilt toward the clearing, zigzagging down a path that was clearer than the way Jordan had come. His sword was in his hand and he had every intention of throwing himself at Clint or the demons or Alex and fighting until they killed him or he won.

His youthful brashness, his total zeal, was the stinging rebuke Richard needed in that moment.

Of course. Of course he was here to fight. Of course he could not just let this happen.

He wasn't sure how Clint had managed to convince him otherwise.

His own sword was in his hand in an instant, and he sprang forward to drive it into Clint.

The warlock waved his hand, and Richard felt air like a wrecking ball in his stomach, throwing him bodily backwards six feet into a tree. The wind knocked out of him, he struggled to stay fully conscious and keep hold of his sword. Empowered by the demonized, embodied evil that was Clint, the demons started to gather physical form. Thunder boomed, shaking the trees, and a wind started to blow in the tops of the pines. Tony arrived, met by Alex with his hands spread and some sort of net forming between them. Richard's eyes riveted on Clint, and he did not watch the scuffle between the younger men.

Clint laughed as the storm wind blew in his clothes and his hair. "You feel that? That is my power stirring. My higher angel. I am dust, and I control dust. I control clouds and rain. I am electricity, and I am thunder. What is your Spirit to compare to me?"

He took a step closer, the shadows of the boys in combat darting around behind him. "The storm is already fierce out on the water, where you sent David and your pathetic cell. You and yours are dead as I speak. You have failed in everything."

He stopped only three feet from Richard and let his voice drop. "This is the end for you, my friend."

"We are not friends," Richard answered.

And summoning all of his strength, he pushed himself off the tree and straight into Clint, driving his sword deep in the man's chest.

Clint stared down in momentary surprise at the place where Richard's blade pierced. Then he began to laugh. It seemed that the blow had no effect, that it did not even stir the demons within this man.

Richard clung desperately to the hilt and tried to push the sword deeper, but he was stopped by some power he could not begin to grasp.

Clint moved his hand again, a motion like brushing off dust, and Richard flew back once more, skin ripping from his hands as he tried to hang onto the sword. The blade disintegrated. He landed on his back in the hard dirt and pine needles.

Tony was still fighting. Alex, it seemed from his combat style, had learned witchcraft from Clint and was eager to use it, but Tony was so fast, so determined, and so bull-like in his style that Alex hardly had the time for the strategic kind of fight he needed. He was just barely fending the teenager off.

Richard's hands stung.

His eyes stung.

He saw Clint advancing on him and told himself it was over for him, but where was she?

Melissa—where was she?

Gone. Gone with the boy.

To do only God knew what.

* * * * *

Mary tried to get up, to get out of David's past and get back to the future where she was sure someone was calling for her, needing her badly, but she couldn't do it.

The link was too strong.

And David, she thought, might be keeping it that way deliberately.

When he came out of his self-chosen coma, a still-young

man with still-fresh losses and pain, Mary was surprised to the point of tears to discover that he was not yet a villain.

Quite the contrary.

The young David woke from his two-year sleep with new hope and new zeal. Looking over what had happened, he determined to know two things: that the Oneness was good and that what he had seen was evil. And knowing that, there was only one choice to make.

His belief, and his drive to act on that belief, were infectious. He became, for the first time in his life, a man of prayer. He sought of the Spirit and connected deeply with the river of personality, purpose, and majesty that it was. He found himself in the Oneness, gloried in it. It lifted him above his losses. Life meant something, something more than it had before the massacre.

His joy impacted Mary, pulling her into it, summoning her to believe with all she was in all the Oneness was, in all the Spirit was, in all they believed to be true. Summoning her to know it to be true. Summoning her to act.

She was at home in this version of David, and more than at home. She was lifted, elevated, made her finer, fuller self. This man could have led a cell in great things. He could have delved as deep as Richard in the things of the Spirit. He could have changed his world.

He had changed his world. But not in the way he now promised to do.

What happened, she found herself whispering, but the whisper was swept off, carried away, buried by the strength of his passion.

She forgot herself in him.

One—and only One.

There were no longer two.

David spent his days with the cell that had rescued him from the hospital. They had all suffered loss, and they grieved together, forming bonds deeper than they had ever known. And David, best and brightest of them, began to form a plan.

It began in prayer. He doubted at first, but over the course of days he became certain that the idea came from the Spirit itself. It was birthed in prayer, after all. And driven by his desire to do right, and to bring the Oneness to the victory they were certainly headed for—the victory promised by the enormity of their defeat in the massacre, a rising again made certain by the distance of their fall.

The conviction that his idea was right, that it was born of the Spirit, did not come immediately. At first he resisted it.

Because it meant going to find the man he had encountered in the woods, and seeing to it that he died or was converted.

Oneness did not take vengeance.

Not normally.

But this time the man was more than just a man. This time he was at the centre of something—something big, much bigger than the massacre. If he was not stopped, worse than those dark days would follow.

More children like his daughter would die.

The demons would triumph.

Little by little, through thought and strategizing and more

prayer, the plan came together. He put in the necessary work. Researched, discovered the man's name and his likely whereabouts. Tracked his habits, his movements. Learned how to find him and most important, how to catch him unawares. In the process he learned more than he had ever wanted to know about the depths of human depravity: the massacre had been the man's first strike against the Oneness, but not—by far—his first crime against humanity.

That they had not stopped him before now seemed a crime.

The plan grew from an idea to an obsession, a heartbeat. He did not tell anyone else. He would need them all—the Oneness would have to do this together. He was certain it would work. But he would wait for the right time to tell the others.

In fifteen days the cell would convene with other cells in a radius of a hundred miles. All the leadership would come, and anyone else who wanted to be there. It was the perfect time, the perfect place.

The Spirit had arranged it that way, he was sure.

It was part of the plan.

The day came.

There were over seventy of the Oneness there. They met not far from Lincoln, in a small town where they rented a hall. It was the first time in several years since the massacre that they had dared to convene like this, in public, but the pogrom seemed to have settled for the time being.

They began in prayer, and it was glorious. So many voices all raised in one, a harmony of sound like waves crashing, like a song. David exulted in it, felt purified and strengthened by it.

When that was done and various members began to speak, he looked across the room and noticed her there. She was beautiful, like she always had been. A small woman, brown hair, courage in every line of her being. Her hair, he saw, was silvered a little. He had heard of her brother's death and was sorry. He had never forgotten the courage of both twins on the night they fled. It had been one of the few threads of gold to which he could cling, and believe that in the end the Spirit would weave a tapestry of their misfortunes that brought beauty out of it all.

Her name was Mary. After his girlfriend, the mother of his child, had refused to follow him into the Oneness, he had sometimes found his heart yearning for that sort of love again—and it was Mary his thoughts most often focused on then.

He was glad she was here.

That too seemed part of the plan.

Finally talk turned to the massacre, and to the steps they were all taking to recover from it, and he knew his time had come.

He stood and cleared his throat, and with the sensitivity of unity they all quieted and waited for him to speak.

"There is a man," he said hesitantly, and thought that was a poor opening. But if he'd memorized a speech, he had forgotten it. This was his moment, and it was too important for memorized speeches.

The Spirit would give him the words to say.

"On the night we ran," he stumbled along, "I encountered a man. A sorceror. He killed several of my fellow runners. And I learned that he set the bombs. He was behind all of it."

Everyone was listening.

"His name was . . ."

And Mary cut him off.

Gently, but with mild reproach she said, "We don't fight against flesh and blood. Our battle is spiritual. I'd rather not know his name and be tempted to hate it."

And that was the end.

No one listened to him after that.

One voice after another chimed in after Mary, some expressing their shared conviction that the fight was not human but demonic; others simply going again into their common stories, the grief, the loss, so they could all mourn together.

But David was done mourning.

He wanted to act.

He needed them to believe in him and to act alongside him, because this he could not do alone.

Once he tried to speak again. But this time they did not notice.

As they all talked, one over the other, no one thought of him again. It was as though he were exiled—not Oneness at all, not now when he needed them most.

And in the depths of his soul Mary stirred again.

She realized, with surprise, that she had been able to see herself—and ached to know how David had viewed her once.

And she knew it now.

This was what she had done.

One gentle rebuke—one interruption.

And somehow he had never found his footing again.

"I'm sorry," she whispered.

And his grip let go.

They were lying on the deck of Chris's yacht.

The sky overhead was nearly pitch-black.

There were demons everywhere.

She was too late.

* * * * *

Melissa held the boy's hand tightly as they pushed their way out of the pine grove and emerged on the cliffs, following a winding path up toward the level ground above. The storm over the water had turned the air a dark, slate gray, and lightning cut it. Wind rushed through the trees and scrub on every side and kicked up yellow sand from the bluffs, marring the air so it was hard to see and harder to breathe. There was no rain as yet.

She wasn't sure what she was doing, really.

She had never felt so torn.

She told herself she was saving the boy. The battle going on in that grove was fierce and dangerous; she was just getting a child to safety. And trying to find the other one, the girl.

So they could both come back to power and heal her again.

Perhaps it was the threat Clint had issued—telling her that she could not imagine how much ground she had already lost. Whatever it was, before the revelation that Richard had set the children free from demonic possession, she had felt no different since her last appointment with the children. But everything had changed when that truth came out. Something deep inside her body, down in her core, had begun to make its presence felt. She could feel it as a tight mass of malignant pressure on one side of her belly, and the more minutes passed, the more it began to send a dull pain throughout her body, a promise of weakness and debilitation to come.

It ached especially in her fingers, where the music was.

That ache, and her growing fear, were driving her just as hard as any concern for Jordan.

She knew that but chose not to acknowledge it as they skirted around a twisted pine that bent over and obscured the path.

"This way," Jordan urged, even though they were already religiously following the path. Melissa had no desire to wander out here longer than necessary. "She's up there. In the cottage."

She paused and looked back over the sea, at the massing clouds and chopping waves. She could not be unaware of the presence in the storm—its darker-than-dark, unnatural personality. Malignant, like the tumor she could feel stealing her life.

Higher angels? She asked herself.

Just an embodiment of human gifts and powers?

Melissa's had not been a life heavily steeped in encounters or battles with the demonic. Not until the cancer, when the demonic offered itself to her as an answer the Oneness could not give. The Mark cell was not her spiritual home; she came from a rural home several states away and had only come to the urban world when her music took her there. She had remained more aloof and separated from the Oneness in Mark than she should have, perhaps. But it was not long after going to the city that the diagnosis had come, and the solution, and all of her questions and fears.

* * * * *

It had taken more than an hour to round up all the kids from the children's home and get them to stay in the cottage, telling them that the storm looked bad and the lightning and wind would be dangerous. Angelica and Susan and the Smiths didn't tell them more than that, even though their warnings produced more disgruntlement and restless annoyance from the kids than anything else.

"But we want to stay outside!" one teen protested. "It's stuffy in here! Just let us stay out until it actually starts getting dangerous."

A thunder clap cut him off, and Valerie Smith gave him a look offering the startling sound as her answer. "There's no lightning yet," he said, sulking.

Angelica had posted herself at the front door. Her sword remained invisible—not good that the kids should see it—but it was ready to appear at any moment.

A smell was beginning to fill the air, mingling with the sea salt. Not the usual smell of impending rain. It was something else, something unpleasant—sulphurous.

"Come on, Tony," she said. "Find him and get back here."

She didn't want to think about what it would mean if Tony didn't find him.

Lightning striking somewhere nearby lit up the sky.

Laughter caught her attention. Two of the kids were outside, dancing around in the dirt driveway with the delight of forbidden fruit. "Get back here now," Susan Brown called, sounding more frayed than Angelica had ever heard her.

Unwilling to leave the woman to her own devices, Angelica stalked into the driveway and collared both kids. They were young, young enough to respect her eighteen years.

"Listen, this is stupid," she said. As though to punctuate her words, thunder clapped deafeningly overhead. It darkened by several degrees simultaneously, and fear flashed in the kids' eyes. "Yeah, that's right," Angelica said. "Now get inside!"

They did, running ahead of her as she returned to her post.

She was only there less than a minute when Valerie appeared white-faced beside her.

"Alicia's gone."

"What!"

"I don't know how she got past us . . . she must have gone while you were out in the driveway."

A few minutes. That was all she'd been gone.

But that was all it took.

**Melissa's heart leaped** when she saw the little girl standing in the path, seemingly waiting for them.

Alicia's light blonde hair was whipped by the wind. She stood unmoving, unsmiling, in the shadow of the scrub pines, the cliff rising to her right and the sea roiling over the drop-off on her other side.

Jordan stopped and greeted her.

She didn't answer.

Only her eyes greeted him back, solemn and unhappy. He ignored it, grabbing her hand and jabbering at her with a bullying, older-brother tone, but Melissa could not share his determination or his indifference.

Yet she needed this child to heal her.

The sky was growing darker by the minute, rapidly turning the day to night. A gust of wind blew, so strong that Melissa had to brace herself against it to stay standing. The sheer drop to the left suddenly seemed terribly close. The wind whipping through the children's hair and clothes made them look vulnerable to blowing away at any minute.

"Come on!" she shouted, fighting to be heard over the wind. "Follow me!"

They didn't respond, and she grabbed both their hands and charged up the path. The focus had shifted—with no need to find Alicia any longer, she felt the urgency of getting both children, and herself, to safety before something unpredictable happened in the wildness of lightning and wind.

And demon, a voice reminded her.

The demonic is the greater threat here.

Dust and pine needles lifted and hurled into the air by the wind half-blinded her as she pulled the children after her. The main path climbed steeply up a sharp bank; it was too steep, too demanding when they were this blind and this buffeted. She looked around hopelessly . . .

. . . and thought she saw a woman beckoning them from another outcropping to the north.

The woman disappeared just as quickly as she'd appeared, ducking away to take shelter, perhaps. But Melissa was sure she'd seen her.

The children were suddenly resistant to her pull.

"We have to go!" she told them. "We have to get where it's safe!"

She hesitated, half inclined to try the steep path anyway, but there she was again—the same woman, beckoning her from another part of the cliffs to the north. And now that she looked, she could see a trail going that way.

She had seen her a little more clearly this time. A woman with long, dark hair streaming in the gale, and a white dress.

The sound of the wind grew higher, taking on tone—like a voice, a voice threatening and a little insane. Without further thought, Melissa charged up the path toward where she had seen the woman.

Jordan tried to pull back. "Not that way!" he yelled.

But she ignored him. If the woman was some kind of enemy, it was too bad; they would have to take their chances. This wind didn't seem discriminating; if they didn't get out of the storm, they'd be blown from the cliffs.

Alicia seemed to agree. She held Melissa's hand tightly and followed her with such sure-footed eagerness it almost seemed like she was trying to pull them both ahead.

The path they were on now was narrow and made more hazardous by roots and the rocky dirt piles left by small-scale landslides, but Melissa kept to it. A flash of lightning lit the vista ahead of them, and she could see now the dark circle of a cave in the cliffs where she had seen the woman. That must be the shelter where she had beckoned them to, and it must be where she was now.

Jordan hung back again. "I don't want to go this way."

Melissa stopped and looked him in the eye. He looked a frightened child—more so than she had ever seen him. Both children had always come to her as children, but confident and clearly gifted, powerful in their own way. That sense of power and confidence was absent from the boy now. Thunder cracked, bringing down a rain of dirt and stones from above, and his face went pasty white.

"It's not safe," Melissa said. "Just trust me. We have to take shelter."

"No," Jordan said, "I want to go back to Clint."

"We can't," Melissa said. "We have to get out of this storm now."

Her timing couldn't have been better. Another ear-splitting crash of thunder dislodged yet more earth from above and from below, and this time the path where Jordan was standing started to crumble away beneath his feet, stones and earth spinning down to the sea below. Melissa, still holding his hand, yanked him forward, and the motion jarred yet more of the ground loose. A rapidly growing gap in the path appeared just where he had been, eating away at the earth. And then the rain began. Stinging, piercing rain.

"Let's go!" Melissa yelled, and this time there was no argument. Both children held her hands and followed her, as fast as they could, almost at a run but wary of the shifting landscape above and below them.

She noticed the smell just before they reached the cave, but she had no other choice. They plunged inside.

She expected to be greeted by the woman she had seen. But instead, they were instantly smothered in total darkness. She could hear dripping in the back of the cave, counterpoint to the downpour outside, echoing oddly. The air was stale, and worse—it stank of something human. But no one seemed to be here.

"I thought she was here," Melissa said.

"Who?" Alicia asked.

"The woman in the path."

Both children just stared at her.

"We shouldn't have come here," Jordan said, his voice trembling.

The realization struck Melissa in a moment: Jordan was this afraid, this timid, because his demon could not act. They were under the shield here.

But she had seen a woman. She was sure of that.

She edged her way deeper into the cave, cautious. "Hello?"

No one answered.

A few more steps, and her foot brushed against something, making her jump. When she did, her hand crashed against something hard—a wall?

No, iron.

An iron lattice of some kind—or bars.

She pushed against them, and hinges creaked. The door swung inward.

Behind her, Alicia's voice was muffled. "This is a torch."

The object her foot had struck. "Can you find matches?" Melissa asked.

One of the children did. In a moment they had lit the torch's oily head, and it flared to life, a blue flame in the darkness of the cavern.

Alicia held it up.

They were at the entrance to what seemed a moderately deep cave, but the narrow opening to the rest of it was covered by the bars—they were bars, like a prison door in some ancient dungeon. It wasn't locked. Taking the torch from Alicia, Melissa pushed the door the rest of the way open and stepped through.

A cavern opened up beyond it, the size of a decent room with a ceiling low enough to touch but just high enough that Melissa wasn't scraping her head along it. Once again she expected to see the woman.

Once again there was no one there.

"Wow," Alicia said.

And Melissa looked to see what she was seeing.

It was the last thing she expected, and it took her breath away.

A painting, etched and mudded and splashed across every wall and the entirety of the ceiling. Rose vines, stretching through scene after scene, face after face, one grand story telling itself across the cave walls.

Jordan stood near the entrance and shivered.

She thought he might have run, if the storm outside had not been so fierce and so terrifying, and he so powerless without access to the demons who gave him strength and significance.

She saw herself in him in that moment. Shivering and afraid of the cancer threatening her from within, unwilling to do without the outside power that had been keeping her alive.

But her eyes were drawn the painting.

To the story it told.

The rose vines led her through it, a path through the tale splashed across the stone. The story of a man—Oneness, she saw—who turned against his own people, who tried to exile a friend, who twisted and changed himself and invited the demons in to help him do it. Who sank himself in their evil to escape what he was. She saw many others in the story—a boy, his bright eyes full of promise and importance, a ship full of Oneness fighting demons over the sea, a man on his knees in prayer.

With a tiny gasp, she saw herself. She was there too, sitting at her piano, playing music while a storm gathered around her.

"Who did this?" she whispered.

A woman's voice answered her. "Her name is April. She is gifted, like you, in the arts—in bringing life into focus and perspective, and seeing and communicating things that reason alone cannot know. And important, like you."

"Why here?"

"She was put here to die."

Melissa swallowed. "Who would . . ."

"The demons would. They fear power like hers. Like yours. They fear this generation of Oneness, because yours is an age of prophets and warriors that few ages have seen. Mine certainly did not."

She turned.

The woman she had seen on the cliff was standing there, lit by a light that wasn't the torch. Her eyes, dark and beautiful, were full of compassion and challenge.

"Who are you?" Melissa asked.

"My name is Teresa."

"You're Oneness?"

She smiled. "Of course."

Melissa looked behind her. Both children were sitting near the entrance, staring out at the pounding rain and the dark. Alicia looked like she wanted to hold Jordan's hand but was afraid to touch him. He was standing outside the iron bars, close enough to get wet by the rain.

"Can they see you?"

"No."

Melissa bowed her head. "You're the cloud, aren't you?"

"Of the cloud, yes." Teresa lowered her voice and looked over the painting again. "I was here when April painted this, watching her remarkable gift. I came to sit with her because I did not know if she was going to die, and I died—long ago—in the same way that they planned to kill her. By starvation, so they would not bear the full weight of such blood."

Melissa couldn't look at her. "They are not 'higher angels,' demons."

Teresa's voice was full of rebuke, but equally full of love. "Of course not."

"I'm afraid," Melissa said.

"Of course you are."

"Why can't the Oneness help me?"

"It can," Teresa said. "But perhaps you are asking for the

wrong kind of help."

"I can't see the good of dying."

"Sometimes," Teresa said, "it is good only because to go on living would be wrong."

Melissa swallowed hard. "Do you know what's happening to Richard?"

"We are not clairvoyant," Teresa said, "or everywhere at once."

"You know an awful lot about me."

"Only because you are here, and like any of the Oneness, I can feel your presence and much of your soul. More so than many, because I want to, and I am not afraid of the depths of pain you feel."

Melissa looked up, finding that her face was streaked with tears. She did not want to talk about herself.

Or about the decision she was making even now.

"What's happening out there?" she asked instead.

Teresa's face was solemn. "A battle. Perhaps the great battle."

"Can I fight?"

"I think you know the answer to that question."

Melissa closed her eyes and tried to think in the direction of another. To send a message without speaking.

Richard . . .

* * * * *

Richard knew, instantly and without shock, that Melissa had broken free.

And his eyes filled with tears, because he also knew what that meant.

Clint was in his face, holding him up by his shirt, suspending him off the ground though he was barely the taller of the two. He was examining Richard's face as though he was an art dealer looking over a particularly pleasing piece before he bought it.

Or more fittingly, an iconoclast looking over a particularly revered statue before he destroyed it.

But with Melissa's change, a link in the chain Clint had carefully constructed broke.

And Richard felt the shift in power.

"Stop," he croaked.

He watched as Clint's eyes widened.

He had intended to deal a blow just then.

He couldn't.

"Put me down," Richard ordered, his voice gaining a little strength. He felt Clint's hand tremour, but he did not obey.

"Shut up," Clint whispered. "Do not speak."

"You have no power to order that," Richard said. "Yours is dominion over the dust. Mine is the power of the word."

He reached up and took Clint's hands with both of his, prying them loose. The warlock's eyes flared with rage.

"Richard!" Tony called from the trees nearby. "I beat him! I'm coming!"

"Do you know you've lost?" Richard asked. "You've been whipping the Oneness with a chain made of dissidents. It's broken. Melissa has turned."

"You never should have learned about her," Clint seethed.

"Funny," Richard said, satisfied to feel his feet hitting the ground. He took a step back from the sorceror. "I thought you had that all under control."

His first word, "Stop," was still holding the man. He did not really understand where the authority to bind him like this was coming from, only that it was his, as naturally his as any birthright, and he believed in it. He clenched his fist, and his sword formed again.

But it was his voice that would conquer.

His word that would be mightier than the sword could ever be.

Tony burst back into the clearing, bloody and bruised but happy, with his lip split and his sword held triumphantly high. "I drove them out!" he announced. "All of them! And the kid's not dead!"

"Impossible," Clint snarled.

"Tony, join me," Richard said. He gave the order in a clipped, no-questions tone. A general now, calling a soldier to his side.

They were facing the enemy incarnate in this man, and he knew better than to think the battle was over now.

Clint's eyes rolled slightly back in his head, and his body trembled—he was breaking free of the power of Richard's word.

"How did you do that?" Tony whispered, awed, as he took

his position next to his commander.

"I don't know," Richard whispered back. "But we are One. And we're not going to lose this fight if you stay close and follow my lead. All right?"

"You got it, Captain."

Dust began to swirl all around Clint, a small storm of its own—a dust devil, Richard thought. Ironic, that old term. Whoever coined it could have no idea how accurate it could be. As the dust gathered, Clint seemed to grow in stature—certainly his strength was returning. What had he boasted? He controlled the earth—the powers of the earth. He was gathering power to himself.

Power that might be stronger than Richard's, untried and untested as Richard's was.

"We have to get him out of here," he heard himself saying, hardly knowing the import of his own words.

"Where to?" Tony asked.

"Where are we?"

Tony, eyes fixed nervously on Clint, said in surprise, "Tempter's Mountain. Where you sent us."

"But not under the shield."

"No, we're too far out."

His mind raced. The whirlwind around Clint was growing in thickness and ferocity, and he knew they had only seconds before he broke free of Richard's order altogether and launched some kind of attack—and this time he would not make the mistake of getting too close. Tempter's Mountain. Angelica was here. Melissa had to be close, and she was firmly on their side now. Even Mary might not be far . . . on a boat somewhere out on the sea, out in that storm. Close maybe, but too far to come to his help.

I can't do this alone, he thought.

A voice answered, You are not alone.

And he knew what to do.

He crouched down. "We have to get him out of here," he said.

"You said that. I'm good with that plan. Just tell me what to do."

Richard smiled. "I don't know what to do. I'm playing this one by ear. But it will work—it has to work."

He remembered Tyler walking out of the basement of the house, using the strength of others to animate his legs.

He remembered whisking over the earth at speeds too high to calculate, all because Clint believed in his own power. Doing things he had never done because he, Richard, did not believe.

And he remembered what he had seen when he brought the children's home people to the mountain.

The hermit's eyes smiling at him.

A man and a woman, both long dead.

The cloud.

He closed his eyes and whispered, "Help us. Get us out of here."

The hermit's voice spoke directly in his ear, so close that he jumped.

"Now that's a good idea."

And more heavily, the old man intoned, "Pray!"

"Tony," Richard said. "Pray."

They let their swords dissolve. They dropped to their knees in the dirt, both of them, let go of their need to fight, let go of the battle, and let themselves be swept up in the rush.

And what a rush.

Richard had never, in all his years of seeking, felt the Spirit like this.

The river was not just flowing in this place; it was flooding at high tide, overturning everything in its path.

In the roar that was prayer, he heard himself telling Tony to reach—to stretch out his hands. They were trying to do what the cloud sometimes did, but in reverse; to cross from their own sphere to the other. To join their brethren on that side of existence that did not belong to them by nature of their own earning but by relationship: because their members, their Oneness, belonged on that side.

He felt like he could hear the hermit urging him on, and laughing hilariously.

The roar of prayer snatched them up, off the earth, into some other place—all three of them.

Clint let out a scream of rage.

They still stood in the grove, but Richard did not think the ground was under their feet. Their surroundings were bright, stark white. He could see the clearing and the trees, and even the storm, through the whiteness as though through a veil. The hermit stood next to him, cackling and rubbing his hands with glee.

"Good boy!" he laughed, slapping Richard on the back. The touch made some impact, but it wasn't—precisely—physical. "Oh, I knew it—I knew you could do it! I tried this, you know, for years. But I could never quite manage it."

Richard could only shake his head in bewilderment—and stare at Clint, who had dramatically changed.

Instead of a young, virile man in the prime of his life, exuding power, the man who moments ago had threatened to destroy them was shriveled, a tiny, wizened creature with large eyes who stared up at them like a cornered animal. Richard had never seen anyone who looked so old—he might have lived two hundred years instead of the twenty-some Clint had claimed. His eyes flicked from one to the other of them, and his body shook—with rage, Richard thought. Behind him, another of the cloud, a big fighter, stood with arms folded and glared down at the little man.

"Patrick!" Tony cried out with joy.

"Hey Tony," Patrick said. "Never thought I'd see you over here before . . . well, you know. Before your time."

"This shouldn't be possible," Richard said.

The hermit waved his hand dismissively. "All kinds of things are possible. Most people just never believe in them enough to try."

"You tried," Richard pointed out.

"I lived alone for thirty years. I got bored. But I didn't quite get up the belief, or the need, I suppose, that you just did."

The hermit fixed his eyes on the hapless sorceror. "Now him, I'm interested to see here. Being on this side doesn't allow for disguises, you see. And now that he's stripped of his, I know him."

Clint—or whoever he was—spat. "Old fool."

"Who are you calling old? Bertoller, they used to call him— Franz Bertoller. And another name before that, I'm sure, and another before that. Responsible for too many things. Too many terrors."

"Why doesn't he have any power now?" Richard asked. "I half-expected the demons to be stronger . . . here. I was only looking for your help."

"The demons have no power in the land of the dead," the hermit said with a sniff. "They only pretend that death is their realm. In reality it is the limit of their power. Beyond life as you have known it there is only the Spirit."

Richard hesitated. "We aren't dead, are we?"

"Of course not. You're just visiting. Like we visit you. And I might add, you're not seeing the fullness of what it's like over here. We, for example, are still appearing to you as you know us. The reality is quite different on this side. But it couldn't exactly be interpreted for you, being as you're still just flesh and blood."

Tony eyed the man they had called Clint warily. "What are we going to do with him?" he asked.

"Shear him," the hermit said, drawing himself up to his full height—which wasn't much. "Strip him of his power and send him back into the world."

"Shouldn't we kill him?" Richard asked.

The question filled the silence that followed.

"He's done so much damage," Richard said. "If we send him back, he'll gather his power again, eventually. Come after us again. Hurt many others besides. Shouldn't we end it here?"

He lifted pleading eyes to his old mentor. "I am asking, not suggesting. I don't know the answer to this question."

"Death always comes eventually," the old man answered. "And with it comes reckoning. But we are Oneness. We offer life. We do not deal death."

The rebuke was gently but firmly given. Richard bowed his head and nodded. He felt Tony's hand on his shoulder.

"I was thinking the same thing," the teenage warrior said.

"Thanks, Tony," Richard said, smiling. "But I can take the sting of that for myself. I've needed to know."

The hermit turned stern eyes on Clint.

"We will, however, administer this. Fool of the devil's, prepare to be stripped of your power."

* * * * *

On the water, the yacht—ceaselessly tossed and swamped by the waves, shuddered, and they felt it.

A wail went up, miserably unhappy.

"Idiots," David mumbled. "They've lost. They should have known they'd lose, turning on me."

Still weak, he lay on the floor of the cabin.

Mary, April, Diane, and Chris, huddled together in a corner across from him, looked at him and then at one another.

The demons had not killed them.

They had shoved them down here instead, intending to wreck the ship. Or so David interpreted their actions.

And instead of taking David with them as their rescued general, they sent him below too.

The traitors, he had raged, the ungrateful, idiotic, slavering curs.

But the demons, for the moment on their own, empowered, and unaccountable to anyone, decided in that moment they would rather have a hive without David calling shots.

"Without me," David said, telling the others as though they would sympathize with him, would take his side as rational creatures, "they are nothing. Without me they're too cowardly and stupid even to finish the work out here. I would have ordered you all killed. They'll let you live because they're afraid of the consequences of killing you."

Now, he sat in the corner where he had been sulking, and he listened to their angry, fearful wails with a mix of satisfaction and anger. "Stupid brutes," he said.

He looked over at the others, and said, "It's because of you, you know." He pointed, leveling a finger—at April.

"You're a Great One, and they're scared spitless of killing you. This is the third time they should have killed you, and they're going to fail again, unless we get lucky and the ship wrecks anyway."

"That's not going to happen," Chris announced. "Whatever's going on up there, I think we're about to lose them. And this is my ship, and I'm going to save it."

"What will you do with me?" David asked. "You've failed at your task. Convert me, right? That's what you were going to do. Well, you haven't. So now what happens to me?"

"We can answer that after we talk to Richard," Mary said.

"Assuming he's still alive. He and Reese. It was dumb of you, to split up."

"They're alive," Mary said. "We would know it if we'd lost them."

"Like you knew it when you lost me?" He sneered.

Mary closed her eyes.

The wails above intensified.

And ended.

A sound like bats' wings rushing out of a cave at dusk sounded from above, and then, suddenly—

Calm.

Chris stood slowly. "I think it's over."

Diane followed, her legs shaking under her. "I don't know how it's possible."

April smiled. "The others must have won somehow."

David only looked away.

As Chris, Diane, and April headed up the narrow stairs to the deck, Mary paused.

"I'm sorry for what happened," she said. "But I did not turn you off the path. You did that to yourself."

He looked shocked.

"How can you . . ."

"Yes, I was there, I went back with you. I felt what you felt. And I will never mock your pain. Nor will I tell you that you hadn't heard the Spirit. But it was your responsibility to do it. You were knocked down, but you refused to ever find your feet again. And I did not do that to you."

She went to the stairs and then turned. "It's not too late, David, to find them again. You are still One of us. We'll help you if you'll let us." His face was turned away, like that of a petulant child demonstrating that he was not listening. "I don't know what we're going to do with you—probably take you back to jail and let you be locked up, maybe even let the administrators of justice administer it all the way. You've killed, David. You've taken lives. We can't protect you from that."

She walked up one step, stopped, and turned one more time.

"I'm sorry," she said again.

He did not turn his face to look at her.

# Epilogue

**Melissa sat in the common room** of the village cell house, her hands clasped in her lap, trying to still a slight tremour—the only sign that she was nervous.

Nick peered at her through the door to the stairs, the only other visible occupant of the house.

Richard stood outside, on the front step. The air had cooled considerably after the storm, as though the pounding rain had robbed summer of its fuel. He looked over the ridge to the bay, sparkling beyond the village in a clear, glorious day.

He wanted to be happy.

Certainly it was a day for it.

And the central event of the day—introducing Melissa to the rest of the cell she was going to call home—was a happy one. She had not wanted to meet them right away. Her own struggle had not ended with her realization, in April's cave, that she could not side with the hive. She had needed time, and space, and asked for it.

Today, they had planned her introduction to the cell in a way that would allow her to bond with each one individually and to know their forgiveness, one by one. They had vacated the house before Richard brought her here, and they would come, one at a time, to sit with her and welcome her.

At least, most of them would.

He smiled faintly at the sight of Mary coming up the road. She carried herself a little differently now—with even greater dignity, if that were possible. Her journey into David's heart had both exposed and absolved her of guilt.

They had delivered David back to jail, along with Clint— though it was unlikely that the police would be able to connect the old, broken man brought to them by the Oneness with the young man they had charged. Alex was in juvenile detention. With Clint stripped of his power, at least temporarily, and David betrayed by the demons he had tried to control, Richard was confident that the hive had been destroyed.

Mary walked straight up to him when she arrived. He smiled at her.

"It's good to watch you coming up that hill," he said. "Like a million times before. Like nothing has really changed."

She nodded, and looked toward the house. "I can feel her presence. I'm glad you talked her into coming."

"She didn't need much talking into. Just a little time."

Mary smiled again, gently, and pushed her way through the door.

He knew she could read his heart—the reasons he couldn't quite be happy today, no matter how much the sun sparkled on the bay, and no matter how much they had won an impossible fight.

Two reasons:

That Melissa had come home, yes, but she had come home to die.

And that Reese had not come home at all.

It had been a week. There was no sign of her, no message, no reaching out. They tried to connect with her through the Spirit, but she was, he suspected, deliberately avoiding them. He was glad Tyler was with her.

Less glad that as far as he knew, so was Jacob.

Their one-time exile had gone renegade, and he did not know why or when she would be back.

"Godspeed, Reese," he whispered, listening to the murmur of voices inside as Mary greeted Melissa and the reconciliation began.

His eyes strayed to the cliff where Chris's cottage was, where the boys had brought Reese after they pulled her out of the sea. He knew Chris was up there, packing his new truck—bought with insurance after the wreck of the old one—to go after her.

Richard wished him godspeed, too, and a homecoming to the Oneness of his own.

* * * * *

*The story continues in Book 4: RENEGADE.*

Rachel would love to hear from you!

*You can visit her and interact online:*
Web: **www.rachelstarrthomson.com**
Facebook: **www.facebook.com/RachelStarrThomsonWriter**
Twitter: **@writerstarr**

# THE SEVENTH WORLD TRILOGY

Worlds Unseen    Burning Light    Coming Day

For five hundred years the Seventh World has been ruled by a tyrannical empire—and the mysterious Order of the Spider that hides in its shadow. History and truth are deliberately buried, the beauty and treachery of the past remembered only by wandering Gypsies, persecuted scholars, and a few unusual seekers. But the past matters, as Maggie Sheffield soon finds out. It matters because its forces will soon return and claim lordship over her world, for good or evil.

The Seventh World Trilogy is an epic fantasy, beautiful, terrifying, pointing to the realities just beyond the world we see.

*"An excellent read, solidly recommended for fantasy readers."*
– Midwest Book Review

*"A wonderfully realistic fantasy world. Recommended."*
– Jill Williamson, Christy-Award-Winning Author
of *By Darkness Hid*

*"Epic, beautiful, well-written fantasy that sings of Christian truth."*
– Rael, reader

**Available everywhere online or special order from your local bookstore.**

# THE ONENESS CYCLE

Exile    Hive    Attack    Renegade    Rise

*The supernatural entity called the Oneness holds the world together.*
*What happens if it falls apart?*

In a world where the Oneness exists, nothing looks the same. Dead men walk. Demons prowl the air. Old friends peel back their mundane masks and prove as supernatural as angels. But after centuries of battling demons and the corrupting powers of the world, the Oneness is under a new threat—its greatest threat. Because this time, the threat comes from within.

Fast-paced contemporary fantasy.

*"Plot twists and lots of edge-of-your-seat action,*
*I had a hard time putting it down!"*

—Alexis

*"Finally! The kind of fiction I've been waiting for my whole life!"*
—Mercy Hope, FaithTalks.com

*"I sped through this short, fast-paced novel, pleased by the well-drawn characters and the surprising plot. Thomson has done a great job of portraying difficult emotional journeys . . . Read it!"*

—Phyllis Wheeler, The Christian Fantasy Review

**Available everywhere online or special order from your local bookstore.**

# TAERITH

When he rescues a young woman named Lilia from bandits, Taerith Romany is caught in a web of loyalties: Lilia is the future queen of a spoiled king, and though Taerith is not allowed to love her, neither he can bring himself to leave her without a friend. Their lives soon intertwine with the fiercely proud slave girl, Mirian, whose tragic past and wild beauty make her the target of the king's unscrupulous brother.

The king's rule is only a knife's edge from slipping—and when it does, all three will be put to the ultimate test. In a land of fog and fens, unicorns and wild men, Taerith stands at the crossroads of good and evil, where men are vanquished by their own obsessions or saved by faith in higher things.

*"Devastatingly beautiful . . . I am amazed at every chapter how deeply you've caused us to care for these characters."*
—Gabi

*"Deeply satisfying."* —Kapezia

*"Rachel Starr Thomson is an artist, and every chapter of Taerith is like a painting . . . beautiful."*
—Brittany Simmons

Available everywhere online or special order from your local bookstore.

# ANGEL IN THE WOODS

Hawk is a would-be hero in search of a giant to kill or a maiden to save. The trouble is, when he finds them, there are forty-some maidens— and they call their giant "the Angel." Before he knows what's happening, Hawk is swept into the heart of a patchwork family and all of its mysteries, carried away by their camaraderie— and falling quickly in love.

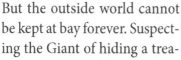

But the outside world cannot be kept at bay forever. Suspecting the Giant of hiding a treasure, the wealthy and influential Widow Brawnlyn sets out to tear the family apart and bring the Giant to destruction any way she can. And her two principle weapons are Hawk—and the truth.

Caught between the terrible truths he discovers about the family's past and the unalterable fact that he has come to love them, Hawk must face his fears and overcome his flaws if he is to rescue the Angel in the woods.

*"A beautiful tale of finding oneself, honor and heroism; a story I will not soon forget."* — Szoch

*"The more I think about it, the more truth and beauty I find in the story."* —H. A. Titus

Available everywhere online or special order from your local bookstore.

# REAP THE WHIRLWIND

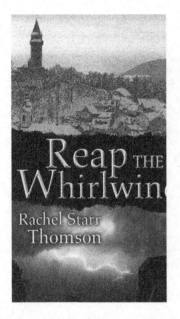

Beren is a city in constant unrest: ruled by a ruthless upper class and harried by a band of rebels who want change. Its one certainty is that the two sides do not, and will not, meet.

But children know little of sides or politics, and Anna and Kyara—a princess and a peasant girl—let their chance meeting grow into a deep friendship. Until the day Kyara's family is slaughtered by Anna's people, and the friendship comes to an abrupt end.

Years later, Kyara is a rebel—bitter, hard, and violent. Anna's efforts to fight the political system she belongs to avail little. Neither is a child anymore—but neither has ever forgotten the power of their long-ago friendship. When a secret plot brings the rebellion to a fiery head, both young women know it is too late to save the land they love.

But is it too late to save each other?

**Available everywhere online.**

# LADY MOON

When Celine meets Tomas, they are in a cavern on the moon where she has been languishing for thirty days after being banished by her evil uncle for throwing a scrub brush at his head. Tomas is a charming and eccentric Immortal, hanging out on the moon because he's procrastinating his destiny—meeting, and defeating, Celine's uncle.

A pair of magic rings send them back to earth, where Celine insists on returning home and is promptly thrown into the dungeon. Her uncle, Ignus Umbria, is up to no good, and his latest caper threatens to devour the whole countryside. He doesn't want Celine getting in the way. More than that, he wants to force Tomas into a confrontation—and Tomas, who has fallen in love with Celine, cannot procrastinate any longer.

Lady Moon is a fast-paced, humorous adventure in a world populated by mad magicians, walking rosebushes, thieving scullery maids, and other improbable things. And of course, the most improbable—and magical—thing of all: true love.

*"Celine's sarcastic 'languishing' immediately put me in mind of Patricia C. Wrede's Dealing with Dragons series—a fairy tale that gently makes fun of the usual fairy tale tropes. And once again, Rachel Starr Thomson doesn't disappoint."*

— H. A. Titus

*"Funny and quirky fantasy."*

Available everywhere online.

Short Fiction by Rachel Starr Thomson

*Available as downloads for*
*Kindle, Kobo, Nook, iPad, and more!*

CPSIA information can be obtained
at www.ICGtesting.com
Printed in the USA
BVOW04s2126291016
466060BV00001B/74/P